Rhubarb Lemonade

Rhubarb Lemonade

OSKAR KROON

HOT
KEY
BOOKS

First published in Great Britain in 2023 by
HOT KEY BOOKS
4th Floor, Victoria House, Bloomsbury Square, London WC1B 4DA
Owned by Bonnier Books
Sveavägen 56, Stockholm, Sweden
www.hotkeybooks.com

A CIP catalogue record for this book is available from the British Library.

ISBN: 978-1-4714-1312-4
Also available as an ebook and in audio

1

This book is typeset using Atomik ePublisher
Printed and bound in Great Britain by Clays Ltd, Elcograf S.p.A.

Hot Key Books is an imprint of Bonnier Books UK
www.bonnierbooks.co.uk

Outside the windows, I see damage from the storm.

It's just me and Mum now. We drift silently through stark corridors.

We pass beaming new parents. We pass frail old folk with empty eyes. They might collapse and die at any moment. A bearded man with a hollow stare is wheeled out of a lift on a bed. Doctors are scurrying, children are crying, fathers are comforting.

Suddenly a cafe, where we can pause.

'Breathe,' Mum says and closes her eyes, though she is far from calm.

Then she drinks coffee. I have a fizzy drink, but wish it was Grandpa's rhubarb lemonade instead.

'I know you miss it and want to go back,' Mum says, nodding at something, but all I see in that direction is toilets.

'To the island, I mean.'

'Yeah,' I reply.

'But Dad really wants to see you. And I've missed you so much.'

It looks like she is about to cry and I can't bear it, but instead she leans forward and pats me on the cheek. I pull back, though I should probably just let her.

'This hasn't been easy on you,' she says. 'Or any of us.'

'Been easy for Dad,' I say, still staring at the toilets.

Sit and talk . . .

'No, my grumpy little darling, not for Dad either.'

'Can you stop calling me darling? Just stop it.'

We are silent for a while. Only the occasional sigh from Mum.

1

'It's been difficult for Dad too,' she says eventually and I just don't get why she insists on always, like, defending him.

'Mm, sure . . .'

'Vinga, please . . .'

'Have you even spoken, you and Dad?'

She laughs.

'Of course we've spoken,' she says. 'Nothing unusual about that. We speak. Pff, of course we speak.'

'OK, good.'

She looks down at the table, offended.

'Good that you speak. Good that it's nothing unusual. Just *great*.'

'Yes, it is.'

We sit a while. Then all of a sudden Mum jumps to her feet – it's time. She lets out a heavy sigh and gives me a big hug.

'Darling,' she whispers.

She just can't help herself. I don't say anything.

Then it's the corridors again, and the lifts and the stairs, but she seems to know the way.

Because she has *spoken to Dad*.

I start telling her about sperm whales, because we have to talk about something. And I'm used to this by now. Talking about the animals deep underwater. Besides, I can't bear to keep thinking about all that other stuff.

Mum might not be listening, but I talk anyway. About how they can survive all alone in the depths of the sea and swim across whole oceans in a matter of weeks and just go about singing sad songs that can be heard for miles around. About how they take care of their young together and help each other.

2

About how they can dive three kilometres down and find their way around in the pitch dark. About how there wouldn't be any seas without them. That the planet would probably stop turning if there weren't sperm whales swimming around it, round and round and round.

'And did you know . . .' I say. 'Did you know that sperm whales have the biggest brains of any animal on Earth?'

Mum is just staring straight ahead.

'Here,' she says suddenly. 'Here it is.'

'But I don't know if they have the biggest hearts, it might be elephants that . . .'

We walk in through glass doors and she sits down on a green chair by the wall.

'I'll wait here,' she says and points to the door that I am supposed to open.

'Aren't you coming in with me?' I ask.

'Best you go in first and I'll join you in a bit,' she says, with a weird expression. Like her face is twitching, maybe from laughter, or tears that aren't coming out properly. 'Let them know. That I'll be in soon, so they're ready for me. Off you go.'

She waves her hand to tell me to go inside but I hesitate. I don't want any of this. Oh god, I just want to go back to the island. To Ruth, Grandpa, the boat, the heat . . .

'Did you know . . .' I say. 'Did you know that a new-born sperm whale weighs one tonne?'

'Go on, Vinga,' she says.

She hugs me tight. Behind her are large windows that look out onto the hospital grounds. Branches and rubbish are strewn everywhere, broken signs and gutter pipes. But in here it is quiet.

Like after the storm. Just a gentle murmur and the occasional child crying in the distance. Footsteps echoing somewhere far away, a coffee machine humming.

Now I'm just going to go up to the door and knock, that's all. That's all.

The Island

The Island

several weeks earlier

In the evenings I sit here on the cliff. I sit here gazing out to sea and waiting for the sun to sink below the furthest point on the horizon. I sit here with my sailor's cap on my head and my heart in the right place. I dream of Aberdeen, of Lisbon and Valparaíso. Of other harbours, elsewhere.

The sea holds so much. In the evening it looks empty, but beneath the surface it is undulating and alive. There are secrets down there. And in the sky. Up there, where dark shadows appear, followed by stars at night. So big, so far away. Beyond comprehension, Grandpa says, then he sighs and looks down at the ground.

'Eternity and infinity.'

Eternity and infinity.

Sometimes I turn around and look at the house. It's no more than a small, square-shaped box. White walls that seem to glow in the evening light of the setting sun. Smoke rising, straight and slow, from the chimney in the roof. Up into that eternity.

Then I see lights on in the windows and I know that Grandpa is pottering around in there. Making tea and rummaging. Humming some old sea shanty.

I sit here on the cliff until the sun has disappeared, taking in the scent and spray of the sea. Then I think about night voyages across oceans and whales sleeping soundly in the dark depths.

About tuna and giant squid. About algae, seaweed, and all the murky harbour districts out there, waiting.

I think about the sailing boat below. The little dinghy lying on the shore among the rocks, awaiting its maiden voyage.

What I don't think about is Dad and Angelica. They're so far away, with their happiness and beautiful balcony full of tomato plants.

The heat out here just goes on and on, day after day, and night time too, which is unusual, and I am constantly clammy with sweat.

Summer is everywhere, scorching and drying everything out. The grass is yellow and dust rises from the ground with every footstep. Everyone is longing for rain. On the radio there are reports of forest fires on the mainland and drought. Old people are having strokes and dying, and suddenly it is illegal to sell disposable barbecues.

I adjust the cap on my head, look at the lighthouse one more time to check its light is shining, then start walking down towards the house.

The light is always shining, but you still have to make sure, Grandpa says.

We don't want any accidents by our island at night, now do we? he says. He has always said that.

Though sometimes, secretly, I do wish for an accident. Because then Grandpa and I would have to row out to rescue the sailors. We would work and sweat all night at sea, and when we came home late the next morning we would stagger up the cliff to the house, and sit and warm ourselves by the fire. Offer the shipwrecked sailors some biscuits and liquor, and

8

they would tell us tales of all their adventures and cargoes and exotic animals and seas and taverns. *Marooned sailors*, I think. *Shipwrecked*. They would point at nautical charts and show us things.

But the light is shining.

No sign of the albatross tonight either.

There never is, but Grandpa saw it once. So he says.

On the last stretch towards the house I'm practically running. Like I'm desperate to just get inside. The twilight birds will have to sing their sad melodies for someone else. For the sea alone.

Here on the island at least everything is as usual.

Here life goes on despite natural disasters and other mishaps on the mainland. Even on a perfectly clear day, there is nothing to see but the horizon. The smoke doesn't reach us here, we can't hear the sirens. Here the old men go about wearing trousers held up by braces and transporting various objects around, as usual. Here they sit side by side on benches smiling at passers-by.

I've always thought they were kind smiles, but now I'm not so sure.

The birds are brooding in Grandpa's birdhouses, as usual, and the lilac blossoms are starting to wither.

'You missed it again this year,' says Grandpa as we sit in the shade of the lilac bush drinking rhubarb lemonade.

He called at some point before school broke up for summer and said: 'It's in bloom now.' Those last few weeks in the city were tough to get through. Mum said I was grumpy and moody, but she was even worse.

Yes, the lilac is withering, but the birds are still singing.

And, as usual, Grandpa takes out his naval chess set every evening after tea and biscuits. He lights his pipe, sometimes pours a drink, but only for himself.

Then he says that when I go home, when I start at that new school, I should be the best chess player in the city.

And I don't tell him that he's the only person I know who even plays chess, or that he might be the only person I know, full stop. I'm trying not to think about any of that stuff about *the new school*.

'Checkmate,' Grandpa says before long. I've still never beat him.

Then it's the weather and shipping forecast. As usual.

People are warned of extreme fire risk in the forest and on the ground; there are already several wildfires blazing and people are being evacuated, bringing only the essentials with them. There is smog over the Bay of Bothnia and North Kvarken, but also high pressure everywhere all the time and a very gentle westerly wind. Good visibility in South Utsira.

Record temperatures.

When Grandpa turns off the radio it is time for bed. Like always. He takes one final puff on his pipe and says: 'Well, that's the day done.'

If there were internet. If I had my phone. Then I would watch or listen to something. But there is nothing but sea outside the window and I think about where I would end up if I just kept going. I lie in bed and flick through Grandpa's nautical charts for a bit, dreaming of islands and islets, skerries and reefs, while Grandpa bustles around in the kitchen. More sea shanties. He is only whistling, but I know the words, about the brig doomed to ruin.

Then I hear Grandpa open the door to go out and fetch more firewood. For coffee and porridge in the morning.

But I never hear him come back. I'm asleep by then.

Yes, on the island everything is as usual.

But not really.

Something about me is different.

And then there's that boat. My sailing boat.

I got the sailing boat as soon as we were left alone on the island, Grandpa and me. We had waved goodbye to Mum down by the harbour and walked home along the beach.

Grandpa had his arm around me, holding me gently in that way of his.

'Alone at last.'

I agreed.

At last.

I had been longing for this for a long time. The thought of summer and Grandpa and the island and solitude was what had made life in the city bearable. On the island again at last.

There is a way home from the harbour via the village, but we almost always take the beach route, unless we're carrying heavy things. It's longer but we don't bump into as many people so Grandpa doesn't have to stop and chat with everybody who comes over and asks questions and pats him on the back. Only the birds are on the beach. Grandpa reels off their names: ruddy turnstone, great black-backed gull, Arctic tern. It's what he's always done.

When we take the beach route we sort of walk round the cliff where the lighthouse stands. Once the harbour and boats have disappeared around the corner there is nothing but a rocky cliff face on one side and sea on the other. And at the top of the cliff is the lighthouse and at the end of the sea is the horizon. I usually take off my shoes and walk barefoot. The small round pebbles feel nice and warm. It kind of hurts, but in a good way: you get summer feet. It's what I've always done.

The house appeared, glowing white, beyond the lighthouse

up on the cliff, and we fought our way up the steep wooden steps. But first we stopped in the middle of the beach and gazed up towards the rocks where Grandpa says there are sometimes seabirds called guillemots. But this time there were only sea mews and gulls, sea mews and gulls.

When we got home, there it was: the package. Plonked on the table, brown and lumpy.

Grandpa hung his sailor's cap on its hook, put his pipe in its dish and coffee on the stove. He nodded at the table and stuffed his hands in the pockets of his suspender trousers.

'Well, open it then,' he mumbled.

The sailor's cap inside the package was just like Grandpa's. Just a tad smaller, and much bluer and newer.

Grandpa looked so pleased, standing there by the stove and beaming. But the real present was the paper.

It was a map.

It looked like a real nautical chart. Wrinkled and crinkled with burnt edges. I sat down at the table and studied it carefully. I knew the way to study a map. Frowning and humming.

Grandpa used to make maps for me when I was little. Back then it was maps of the garden, which almost always ended under the lilac bush where he had left me a licorice pipe or some other treasure.

I sat there for a while pretending to think hard, so as not to disappoint Grandpa. And to give him time to finish his coffee. He can really draw, my grandpa. Brigs and waves and gulls and fish. When I was little he drew tattoos on me in Biro and I cried when the anchors and seagulls washed off the next time I went swimming in the sea. He doesn't even ask me if I want tattoos any more, but he is obviously still drawing maps.

This one showed the island from above and the sea around it. There were big waves in the water and a ship sinking far out to sea. It was being pulled into the deep by the long tentacles of an enormous octopus. On the island the map showed the harbour and the village. The Great Wood, our house and woodshed. It showed the cliff and the lighthouse and the beach down below.

There was the X. The treasure.

On the beach, below the lighthouse. We had just walked past it.

'Wasn't sure if you might be getting too old for this type of thing,' said Grandpa without turning around. I said nothing. I wasn't sure either. I probably *was* too old for this type of thing, but I didn't feel it. Not deep down.

'Are you coming with me?' I said eventually.

He nodded happily. With his eyebrows raised.

Before Grandpa could put on his sandals and cap, I was already out by the woodshed. Without even stopping to say hello to the sheep grazing beyond the shed, I hurried straight down towards the pebbly beach. The sheep stared at me a while before continuing their never-ending chewing.

I was *not* too old for this type of thing.

Halfway down the steps I had to stop and wait. Then I saw him at the top, Grandpa.

'Off you go,' he called. 'I'll follow.'

So I was all alone when I got to the spot beneath the lighthouse. Already from a distance I could see that there was something there. A boat. A wooden boat. A sailing boat? It was lying a little way up against the rocks and we had walked down by the water's edge on our way home, so I hadn't seen it then, or just hadn't thought about it – but now it was all I could see.

I was just standing there and staring when Grandpa caught up. I had no idea what was going on.

'It's yours,' he said shortly.

'Mine? You mean the boat?'

'I mean the boat.' Grandpa nodded.

'Really?' I asked.

'Really.' Grandpa nodded again.

It was a little dinghy, he said, and it was mine, but before I could take it out sailing I had to make it seaworthy. Lying next to it were sails and a bunch of different poles and ropes.

In front of the thwart, where you sit to row, was something like a plank with a hole in it. That's where you put the mast, Grandpa said. But the sail needs mending and the hull needs sealing, scraping, sanding, painting. New ropes and fittings.

It would be quite a job to make it seaworthy, he said. But if I wanted to . . .

'I want to!' I shouted. I couldn't believe it.

I ran round and hugged Grandpa so hard and so suddenly that he dropped his pipe somewhere among the pebbles.

Mum and Dad thought it was weird that I wanted to stay with Grandpa on the island for so long. I thought it was weird that they didn't get it.

'But what are you going to *do* there all summer?' said Mum. 'What if it just rains the whole time?'

But they have nothing to worry about. I've got plenty to do now. I spend day after day on the beach with my boat. And there's no rain.

At first, Grandpa would come and help me. We brought down tools and planks, scrapers and brushes. He had already ordered and bought things from the shop; lots of pegs and plugs and stuff that he'd been keeping hidden in the woodshed. And he had fashioned his own tiny little objects out of wood but I had no idea what they were for. He had to show me everything that needed doing and where all the little bits were supposed to go.

And one morning Grandpa walked over to see his neighbour, Ylva the sheep farmer.

Ylva wears trousers with braces, just like Grandpa's, except green. She has grey hair tied in a bun on her head and long, crooked fingers. She is Grandpa's best friend, she always says, and hugs me a little too hard.

Then later that day Ylva came driving along the beach in her tractor and helped us to lift the boat onto some logs so we that we could access the whole body to scrape it all over.

Ylva said that she would love to join us on its maiden voyage, but would never impose on something that should be just ours.

Now I'm usually alone down here on the beach. I know what needs doing. Mainly scraping and sanding.

Sometimes I wonder what to do with the sail. Then I unfurl it across the pebbles and inspect it. There are big rips in it and a large hole where it's supposed to attach to the mast. It is then that the maiden voyage feels very far away. But in my dreams I can picture myself sailing the boat, with my sailor's cap on my head and the rudder in my hand. I see myself sailing around the entire island before heading straight out towards the horizon. I have a packed lunch with me. And an anchor tattoo on my arm.

Sometimes Grandpa comes down with a picnic basket. Then we sit on the stones and eat sandwiches with fried egg or cucumber. We gaze out to sea and sometimes Grandpa tells me about boats that have come and gone.

'It might look calm now, but these are dangerous waters,' he says. That's what he's always said.

He points here and there and tells me about rocks and reefs hiding beneath the surface. But I see only water, calm and still.

Then he lights a pipe and lies down on the pebbles. Sometimes he pulls his cap over his eyes and sleeps.

Before Grandpa leaves he runs his stout, sturdy hand over the parts I've sanded. And he nods.

You have to know how everything works. You have to know exactly where each chock goes to get the right result. And it has to be this very specific kind of chock . . . It's so precise. The curve of the boat isn't for beauty's sake. It is beautiful *because* it's the best shape to allow the boat to float and move smoothly on the water.

Its beauty lies in the fact that it is functional and adapted to the elements. Grandpa's words. I just nod and agree.

Otherwise, if it's not to do with boats or birds, he really doesn't talk much.

He mainly just hums, sings, and laughs from time to time. This suits me fine. He never insists on asking loads of questions. As far as he's concerned, everything just is what it is.

Grandpa always wears his sailor's cap, all year round; it is sun-bleached and smells of pipe smoke and the sea. He wears a chequered shirt and trousers with braces and large pockets. Boots. When it's cold he puts on a blue jacket with a collar and gold buttons. It might look stylish if it weren't for the tattered sleeves and his shirt poking through the holes at the elbows. If it's hot, like this summer, he swaps his boots for a pair of brown sandals.

He has always looked the same, Grandpa. Or as long as I've known him, at least, which is basically the same thing.

Grey hair sticking out in all directions, even though he's always trying to smooth it down with his hand. Sometimes I suggest he tries using a comb but he just scoffs. In his pocket: pipe, tobacco and a small red pencil. He uses the pencil to mark planks for sawing or if he has a crossword to do. In spring he uses it to write labels, labels that he puts up on sticks in the garden: broad beans, carrots, parsley. Swirly, wavy, almost unreadable . . . he writes like the sea.

Sometimes Grandpa wears binoculars around his neck and keeps a chequered handkerchief in his shirt pocket. On his arm he has a memento from South America: a half-faded anchor tattoo.

Sometimes he has sharp little beard bristles on his cheeks. I used to rub my palm over them and feel them tickle. That was when I was little. Sometimes I want to do that now too, but I'd feel too silly. He has thick curly grey hair on his arms, all the way down to his hands, even a bit on his fingers. And wild eyebrows above his dark eyes. If he pulls the hairs down they almost reach the tip of his nose.

My grandpa is a sailor who has come ashore. If you can even call this 'ashore', living on a clifftop in the middle of the sea.

Anyway, he has barely left his island since he *came ashore*. We've always been the ones to come here and visit him.

Mum, Dad and me.

Now it's just me.

Sometimes I think about that day when we waved Mum off. I think about how me and Grandpa were both like, at last – just the two of us. I think about that day and remember the cap and map and boat.

And that's all fine. But still.

Still, I think about Dad a lot. I think about his brand new life. And that if it weren't for his brand new life I wouldn't be allowed to stay here alone for so long. I think about the new room that is supposed to be 'mine', though I've never seen it and don't think I want to. I think about Angelica and the way she talks to me and the scarf and its smell.

And I think about the hug Dad gave me before Mum and I set off for the boat. How long it lasted. And how tight he held me. Like he never wanted to let go. And I think about the look in his eyes afterwards. Sad, moist eyes. It was by the car, outside the gate. The car that used to be Dad's too. The gate that he used to pass through to come home. Now he was just a guest.

And I think about him saying: 'Farewell, Vinga.' It sounded so formal. Like I was about to sail around the world and never come home again.

He should have just said 'Bye' and given me a normal hug. 'Have a great time,' he should have said, and then hurried off, a bit stressed. That would have been normal. But I remember him standing there and watching us drive away. With his arm raised until we disappeared around the corner of the park and headed for the coast.

That was not normal.

I do talk to Dad sometimes. But to Mum more. We go

over to Ylva's to borrow her house phone. Grandpa refuses to get one – he says there's a reason people come to live on islands – and my mobile doesn't work out here. Maybe if I climbed all the way up the lighthouse and leaned far out, but that doesn't seem like a great idea.

And who, other than Mum and Dad, would I talk to? Dad always sounds so happy when I call. I hate that he sounds so happy. He says that he is doing well but he is pining. He doesn't say for who or what and I don't dare ask. He says that Angelica is also doing well, even though I don't ask and don't care. Then he says that he misses me. To which I just say 'ah' or 'mm', although I really wish I could say more.

Sometimes I miss him so much it hurts.

Mum never sounds happy, though I can tell she's trying. She asks how I am and then says everything is going to be just great when I get home. That at least my normal bedroom will be just the same and we'll do loads of fun things in the autumn. And she promises that everything will be better in my new school. Even though she can't really promise that.

I hate that she sounds so sad.

Then she wants to talk to Grandpa for a bit as well. So I sit there in the kitchen with Ylva and she asks me about the boat and school and Grandpa and the city and all that. Really, I'm trying to listen in on what Grandpa is saying in the other room, but all I hear is 'yes, no, sure, mm.'

On our way back from Ylva's, Grandpa is much more talkative than usual.

I think he is trying to distract me, but it all feels like stones in my shoes.

Like stones.

'You can get used to anything, except a stone in your shoe.'

That's what Grandpa always says, when something is wrong. He said it a few times this spring when I spoke to him on the phone.

He never said all that crap about everything turning out great, but he did say that you can get used to anything. Sometimes I had to add in the bit about the stone myself.

Sometimes at night I think a lot about Dad leaving. That he has already left. For ever. Then I cry, as quietly as possible, and can't get to sleep. Then I force myself to snap out of it and think about the boat instead. But Dad pops up again. With Angelica and her belly and the way she speaks to me like I'm a little kid. The way she calls me by names that I never gave her permission to use.

And Grandpa just snores. Our bedrooms are only separated by a curtain.

At times like these, when I can't sleep, I fantasise about the port of Lisbon and coming ashore after serving on a great big ship. I'm wearing my sailor's cap and have a kitbag over my shoulder. A pipe in my mouth and a fist in my pocket. I think about walking along the quays looking for Sally Jones. And I find her in O Pelicano Bar where we sit all night long and she tells me tales from the Indian Ocean and Bay of Biscay. From the North Cape and Gulf of Finland. And Fidardo takes out his accordion and Ana Molina sings . . .

They can be pretty ridiculous sometimes, these fantasies, but so what? They're fun. And they just keep coming, all these thoughts and dreams about what is to come. Sometimes it feels like all I ever do is wait.

Wait for the wind to come and carry me away.

I know Dad thinks it's sad. He even told me so. I suppose he wants a sunny, happy child, but what he doesn't understand is that I love my daydreams, no matter how silly they are.

'You can't just keep planning what you're going to do years from now,' he says. 'You have to live in the here and now.'

'*Carpe diem*,' I say back, hoping he will realise how ridiculous he is being and get embarrassed, and maybe he does a little, but he still carries on:

'I just mean . . . you're still a child, you should be enjoying yourself. Soon you'll be grown up and then . . .'

As if everyone under the age of eighteen is blissfully happy all the time.

Anyway, I dream what I like and I dream myself to sleep there in the house on the island, and I keep dreaming and wake up later and think only of the boat below the lighthouse.

Then everything is fine and Grandpa is already sitting at the table and calling to me.

'Rise and shine, sea dog!'

I don't like being called sea dog, but I'm used to it. Then we eat porridge.

Down on the beach there is a strong smell of rotting seaweed. The sun is blazing, as usual.

You can get used to anything, except a stone in your shoe.

On Wednesday evenings it's the pub down in the village. Grandpa says we have to go or people will talk. He comes down to the boat to get me. He inspects and feels and nods and hums.

'It'll be really something, this boat,' he says. 'Good work, captain.'

I love it when he calls me captain. It's what he has always called me and I'm not too old for this sort of thing. Not now anyway. Not here.

Up in the house Grandpa gets changed. He takes off his braces, trousers and shirt. They end up in a pile on the floor. He's only going to wear them again, he says. Then he walks around in nothing but his underpants for a bit. I look at his muscular sailor's body and think that's the way I want to look. All tough and weathered.

But I know I'm different.

Then he, Grandpa, wanders around pretending not to know what to wear. And I say 'the sailor suit' and he says 'no'. So I say 'the navy coat' and he says 'too dirty'. Then I say 'the royal cape' and he says 'too fancy'. And I say 'the ball gown' and he laughs.

Then he takes out his one and only suit.

It's hanging up in the same place it has always been, under the stairs to the loft. With a white shirt and spotty tie. Every Wednesday it's the same. He takes out his good shoes. Then he ends up wearing his sandals anyway. He says the shoes are 'too damn showy'.

'No point being all shiny for no reason,' he says.

And the tie stays where it is. He says the tie isn't going to make an appearance until his own funeral and that's just going to have to wait.

'Promise,' I say, and Grandpa says he will try his best.

The village is just a small cluster of houses, down by the harbour. We don't bother cycling and go by foot, otherwise Grandpa gets all wobbly on the way home. We live at the furthest possible point from the village, the longest distance and the steepest climb, next to a sheer drop down to the sea and eternity.

We walk along the gravel road, past the lighthouse and sheep grazing all around.

The Great Wood is really only a small grove of trees. The birds are singing softly there as the sun is slowly setting. Grandpa whistles back to the trees and reels off the names of the birds. It's what he's always done.

As far as I'm concerned, Grandpa has always been here. Always been the person pointing out and naming the birds and the trees. Always been so disappointed that I never remember their names. But there are so many of them, the hawks and sparrows and swallows. The rowans and aspens and hazels. Can't they be just birds and trees?

Then there's Ylva's farm and the hill sloping down to the village and harbour. From there the view of the sea and horizon spans on all sides. And you can hear the sounds of the pub. It's an old barn on the edge of the village, just beyond the cemetery where sailors are buried in rows. Now the barn is filled with tables and benches, and colourful lamps hang from the ceiling. Ylva stands behind the bar and serves beer. I have an orange soda and it makes me think of Dad. But only for a second.

When you go to the pub you sit on a bench and drink beer and eat peanuts. Other people are sitting all around you doing the same thing and you talk to them. Or you just stay quiet. I mainly stay quiet. When your glass is empty you look around to see if anyone else's glass happens to be empty. Then you go to the bar and buy more for whoever needs or wants it. At the bar you have a little joke with Ylva who calls herself a bartender.

Music plays in the background, but it's mostly just guitars and men singing about love. Hardly any proper sea shanties.

After a long evening in the pub your legs might go a bit funny. Some people look like they're swaying as they walk. That's just because they didn't eat enough, Grandpa says with a smile.

At the pub lots of people come over to our table. Mostly old men who want to chat to Grandpa. They always start by saying something to me: first how much I've grown, then they ask about the sailing boat, or the 'boat build', as they say. They usually try to be funny.

'Must be boring hanging around with this old fogey all summer, right?' they say and then they look very pleased and sort of light up when they hear my short answer. Boring? No way.

But it's really Grandpa they want to talk to. So I go and have a little wander round.

Sitting in the far corner is a girl that I've seen on the island before. Down by the boat, when we waved goodbye to Mum. She is wearing a black hat and shiny black jacket and she looks lonely and bored surrounded by all these old men. We're probably about the same age, but she pretends not to see me. Or maybe she really doesn't notice me.

Which wouldn't be unusual.

Strange though. I should be pretty visible. With my curly

bright red hair and all these freckles. With my fat lips and spindly legs. Dressed in baggy Hawaiian shirts and red rubber boots. Weird that I often seem to be invisible.

When I was little, I would think quite a lot about not existing. I would sit on the Big Rock up in the woods and try to disappear. But try as I might, I never did. And when I came back home no one had even missed me all that much. They just said hello as usual and continued emptying the dishwasher, reading the paper, hoovering the hall.

At school, same thing. I've always felt separate from everything going on around me. Like no one has ever needed me there. And the times I've been home sick, or just called in sick, and stayed at home watching TV or listening to something, no one missed me.

Now the sea is my only refuge. You can really disappear at sea. Go missing and be missed.

When I come back to the table, where Grandpa is sitting surrounded by old men, I see one of them lean back in his chair and sigh.

'Poor girl,' he says, before gathering up a few empty glasses and going to the bar.

The others go quiet when they notice I'm back. Grandpa smiles, but I know I've caught them in the act. I know it was me they were talking about. I am the 'poor girl.'

Grandpa sways on the way home and he says that same thing about not eating enough. We walk arm in arm and look up at the stars.

'Eternity and infinity,' he mumbles. 'Now they're lighting their cigars. Eternity and infinity.'

Then he says loudly:

'Isn't it incredible to think that you and I, of all the possible people in the world, are the only ones walking here right now? The odds of us being exactly us, here, now?'

'Anything else would have been equally incredible,' I say.

Then he sighs again, smiles and nods. Then he begins to sing:

What fun we had at the party,
How I wish I could have stayed there.
The music and liquor were hearty
And I think we both had our share.
Oh, to sleep, to rest and dream,
Tonight it took a long while . . .

Ruth

Then suddenly she's just standing there.

It's a day or two after the pub and everything is as usual, with the blazing sun and dripping sweat and heavy, pressing air. The eternal sea slowly rises and rolls ashore, glittering. The wildfires on the mainland have spread and there are helicopters bombing them with water. Holiday makers are having to flee their summer getaways. But here all is calm and still. It's like the island is in its own glass dome. You listen to the radio and imagine the world out there. A world where forests are burning. A world where pregnant bellies swell and abandoned mothers clean out their wardrobes. Where fathers calmly water their tomatoes. You can look to the horizon and hope there's something there, or not. But right here, right now, there is nothing to hope for. There is only me and my boat and the sun and waves and Grandpa and the occasional bird and pebbles being slowly dragged into the sea.

And now, suddenly, there is her.

I was so absorbed in my work on the boat that I didn't hear her coming. She is a shadow, almost hovering in the heat.

'I've seen you around,' she says.

I don't know how to respond. Don't people usually start with a 'hello' or something similar? I just stand there, staring. Being alone is so easy. When I'm alone I really couldn't care less about how I look or what's going on inside my head. I am just me and that's OK. It's the same with Grandpa. He knows me and when we're together I can just be. But now here I am with this girl all dressed in black looking me up and down.

Examining me, with disappointment, almost disgust. And immediately I see myself from the outside, through her eyes. I see an idiot who can't speak.

She looks at me like I'm really weird.

I probably am.

She looks at me like I'm a rare animal. A fringe-finned fish, a deep-sea anglerfish. Sweat trickles and tickles my skin.

She is barefoot. She is wearing a long black vest top and a big black hat that hides half her face. I probably would have found her frightening from a distance, but now she is right up close.

I stay quiet. So bloody quiet.

Sometimes it's so hard to open my mouth and speak. Everything I say sounds so silly. Until I get used to the sound of my own voice, I guess.

Eventually I squeeze out a 'Hi', but it barely even sounds like a hi.

'What are you doing?' she asks.

Then she raises her eyebrows and does a sort of rolling gesture with her hands to show she is waiting for an answer. It's my turn now. But my tongue just ties itself in knots so I look down at my feet getting burned on the sun-drenched pebbles and I think it's good to toughen up the skin. I stay still as long as physically possible. Until it feels like my skin is about to set on fire, as if my whole self is about to burst into flames . . . But then I look up and see her tired eyes, sour face and sharp nose. And then I have to move my feet and kind of dance on the spot before getting them in the shade of the boat, and at that moment it feels like something inside lets go and words start gushing like a river.

34

'Well, I've got to make this boat seaworthy, so I'm sanding it now to oil it later, and then I have to make holes here and here, and fix the shroud, and I have to make sure the spiritsail is whole, and the rig is steady, and then there's a lot to do with the rudder, as you can see, and I'll attach a new chock here and here, and make compartments here where I can keep my lunch box and nautical chart – well, that's if there's even time for a maiden voyage before I go back to the city, and . . .'

Now she's the one staring in silence.

Then I get embarrassed and turn away to start sanding again, even though this bit of the boat doesn't really need more sanding. I try to appear indifferent. I hope she goes away. I hope she stays. Hope she goes, hope she stays.

'I hate boats.'

I stop.

'What?'

'I hate boats. I hate islands. I hate the sea. Just hate it.'

I tip my sailor's cap, hold out my hand and introduce myself.

'My name is Vinga and I'm going to be a sailor.'

Then she laughs and says:

'Ruth. My name is Ruth. I'm going to be . . . famous for something cool, I reckon.'

That evening I sit up on the cliff, as usual.

There's this feeling in my belly. It's sort of messy and doesn't make any sense, but it feels good. Like a tickling and fluttering inside me and I can't lose myself in the sea like I usually do. It's like I want to laugh but it refuses to come out properly. It just bubbles away inside. Like those little silver-glittering fish that frolic and dart below the boat dock. Or like those sparks that spit out of Grandpa's fireplace. The type that could set fire to a whole forest on the mainland. I can't make up my mind whether it feels nice or not. It's like a happy anxiety.

As usual, I am gazing at the sea and setting sun. As usual, I am alone. As usual, I hear a few birds singing from the bushes by the lighthouse and the waves rolling onto the pebbly shore. As usual, I feel the spray of the sea. Breathe in its scent. As usual, sea turtles are swimming along and singing their songs somewhere down in the depths, in search of the perfect beach and the fullest moon. But all that is elsewhere. None of it reaches me this evening. Just for this evening, I don't dream myself away. Just for this evening, I am right here. I'm not thinking about waves and wind forecasts. Or seedy harbour districts and parrots on shoulders. Just for this evening, I think about what happened today.

The sight of blazing sunshine and used sandpaper. The scents of wood and sea. A figure in black sat huddled in the furthest shadows of the rocky cliff. Wide sun hat low over her eyes. Her – the girl who hates the sea. The girl called Ruth. The girl who makes my insides feel like a fire spitting sparks.

How did this happen?

She sat there for a long time and watched me working on the boat. Occasionally she would ask something and I answered. Occasionally I asked something. Sometimes I just wished she would go away. Being alone is so much easier. But she didn't.

She is staying with her granny on the island. For a few weeks. She usually lives in the city too. Her granny runs the shop and Ruth helps out sometimes.

'It's OK,' she said. 'Quiet.'

'Good to have something to do,' she said later. 'It can get pretty boring here otherwise, huh?'

Then I ran my hand over the boat. As if to say: how would I know? I have plenty to do.

And she just sighed.

Then we were both silent.

I felt a bit silly. Even kind of ashamed of my sailor's cap. Then I felt ashamed of being ashamed of something that I love so much and was a gift from Grandpa. I was ashamed of my pale, blotchy legs and massive red hair. The freckles dotted all over my body. My favourite shirt covered in bright colours and palm trees. I felt like a silly little kid.

And she just sat there, so cool and sure of herself. Dark and quiet, with her straight nose, dark eyes and black hair flowing out from her hat and over her cheeks.

She didn't seem to mind silence. But I felt I had to speak, even though I didn't want to and didn't know what to say. I thought for a long time and eventually asked her if she knew who my grandpa was. I regretted it the moment I said it. Couldn't I come up with something better? Why the hell did I ask her that?

How is it possible to be so secure and so insecure at the same time?

'Everybody knows him,' she said.

Back to silence.

'He's kinda quirky, huh?' she said after a while.

I had almost forgotten she was there. I was fiddling with the rudder fitting. Have to get it straight.

'Mm, who?' I said.

'Your grandpa. He's a bit weird.'

I didn't know what to say to that. It kind of pissed me off. So I kept banging on the rudder fitting in silence.

But later we found ourselves sitting with our backs leaning against the boat. We sat there side by side and talked. About schools and streets and parents and friends. Dreams. And it just, like, flowed.

We found out we're the same age but that's about all we have in common.

She likes the city; I dream of sailing out to sea. She wishes for fame; I want to disappear. She seems cool and popular; I'm a nerdy, quiet loner. Her hair is black and mine is red. She hates life on the island, while I am happier here than I've been in a long time.

Then she had to go home. She seemed kind of grumpy, but it's not like anyone was forcing her to hang out with me all day if I was so boring.

Just as she disappeared up the cliff and beyond the lighthouse, Grandpa appeared, walking from the other direction. That was enough sanding for one day, he said. Now it was time for a good meal.

He had caught a couple of plaice. Except he calls them flatfish.

Then he checked the rudder fitting.

'You don't have to bash it in so darn hard,' he said.

When I wake up in the mornings, Grandpa has already been up for ages. He'll be sitting at the kitchen table with his hands wrapped around a mug. Listening to the radio and looking out the window, at the sea and sky. There's a popping, crackling fire in the stove, and the porridge is ready and waiting.

Sometimes Grandpa does a crossword. He rests his head in his hand and furrows his brow. Taps the pen on the table, thinking. Sometimes he sits there whittling something. A new hook, a spoon, a handle for some tool. He can whittle practically anything. He sharpens his crossword pencil with a knife.

And when he sees me peeking out from behind the curtain he lights up and smiles. Then he gets up and ladles out some porridge. Serves it up and makes it nice. Asks if I want some coffee. Though I never do.

'Any dreams?' he'll ask.

Then I usually just make something up. I never really remember my dreams but I think they're usually about fathers disappearing or houses and trees going up in flame. Because sometimes I wake up in the night drenched in sweat. But I never tell Grandpa.

I make up ocean voyages instead. Huge ice bergs and wild storms.

It sounds better.

Grandpa has a whole woodshed filled with tools. He has built practically everything in his house himself. Beds, tables and chairs. Chests, benches and cupboards.

He shows me how to use his carpenter's workbench.

'There are a few things for the rig that you'll have to bring up and file down,' he says. 'And we'll need new fittings to fix the mast hoops.'

The fittings are impossibly small. But Grandpa shows me a tiny little screwdriver in his big strong hands. And he clamps one of the hoops tightly onto the workbench, takes out a bracket and the teeniest screws I've ever seen. They are swallowed up between his fingertips. He wiggles his hand a little, and it's in.

'There,' he says simply. 'Now you know how.'

Hardly.

Then there are ropes and rope end caps.

'We've got some we can use,' he says. 'But we'll have to go down to the shop one day and order some smaller end caps.'

Then she appears again.

I imagine Ruth in the shop dressed in a cap and apron just like her granny wears. I imagine her writing our orders down on a piece of paper, saying no problem, sticking the pencil stub behind her ear, leaning over the counter . . .

'And we already have plenty of oil here.'

Grandpa interrupts my thoughts. He is standing in the corner by a shelf full of paint tins, picking and pointing.

'You go down and carry on with the boat. I'm going over to Ylva's for a chat.'

We tip our sailor's caps to each other and say goodbye. He promises to come down later to inspect my work and bring me some rhubarb lemonade.

I've been here working for ages. Grandpa lent me a gimlet and I've been struggling to bore these new holes for the shroud. It's hard, sweaty work, but I like the smell of the wood shavings as they're screwed out in long spirals. I've turned around to look down the beach a few times, but the only movement is from the air itself, sort of quivering in the heat. She said she would come, but that's the kind of thing people just say and don't mean. Why would she come? Thoughts dance through my head as I screw the gimlet deeper and deeper into the wood.

Coming, not coming. Hope, don't hope.

She's already managed to ruin everything, Ruth. I don't know why I care. Life on the island is supposed to be easy. Just me and Grandpa and the occasional old man in trousers and braces. But now there's something else as well.

I make my mind up to forget about her, carry on with my summer as usual, me and Grandpa, the boat, Wednesday nights at the pub, the birds, the sea . . .

And just then I hear a hooting sound from high on the rocks. The first thing that comes to mind is the albatross. Is that what it sounds like? I turn to look at the cliff and lighthouse, but I am so blinded by the sun that I nearly fall backwards. I have to move and look from the side. Pull my sailor's cap as far down my forehead as I can.

Then I hear it again. And I see something black fluttering up on the rocks. Halfway up to the lighthouse. Something big. But before I can really figure out what it is – my brain works so slowly – I hear laughter.

Ruth.

How did she get up there? It looks super dangerous. The cliff face below the lighthouse is vertical, just a sheer drop down to the pebble beach. I have never, even when I was little, thought of trying to climb there. And never seen anyone else do it either.

But there she is. Sitting there, howling with laughter.

She probably thinks she startled me, that I was scared. But I wasn't, was I? Just a little curious, maybe, and you can't blame me for that.

After all, it might have been a rare animal. And I suppose it was.

I try to stay cool and calm as I approach the cliff, but my heart and thoughts are racing. These stubborn, sticky thoughts. What do I say now? What will we talk about? Last time she acted like my company was boring as hell, so what's she even doing here?

'How did you get up there?' I ask anyway.

I have to yell so she can hear. She must be fifteen metres above me. Sitting on a jutting rock that looks barely big enough for a seagull, let alone a person. It feels like I'm just shouting at a cliff face.

'I didn't,' says the voice from above. 'I got *down*!' She points up.

Directly above her is the highest point of the cliff. Where the lighthouse stands.

'Thought I'd try a shortcut,' she says.

'Thought you'd risk your life, you mean?' I say.

Then she narrows her eyes at me, spins around on her little platform and starts to climb. Quickly and nimbly, she climbs down. Like a lizard scuttling along the rock face. I can't even begin to fathom how her feet get purchase on those tiny bumps of rock, hopping from one invisible foothold to the next. How her luminous, bony little fingers manage to cling to those tiny crevices is incomprehensible. She presses her body up against the rocks and sort of flows. Suddenly she is directly above me. If I reached out I could almost touch her bare foot. But she quickly turns round again.

And jumps.

There is a rattling sound as she lands and she does a few rolls over the stones, just like superheroes do in movies. I think she must have broken a bone or something. At least.

I want to rush over to comfort her, check she's OK, call for help, but before I know it she is standing right in front of me. She looks kind of grumpy and bored, like nothing happened, and says hi.

Apparently an ordinary 'hi' isn't too much to ask this time.

But she is anything but ordinary.

'I do it back home. In the city.'

'Do what?' I ask.

'Climb. A few times a week I go to this place with climbing walls and I train. I'm gonna be in the Swedish Championship this autumn. So now I've got to train here.'

Sure, I think, but presumably she normally has ropes and stuff. And coaches. And soft mats to fall on.

Ruth comes over to the boat to see what I've been doing. She picks up a few of the spirals of wood shavings. She holds a bunch of them in both hands. Then she takes off her hat, puts it down carefully in the boat, and pours the

45

shavings onto her head so that they get stuck in her long shiny black hair.

'Now we look more alike,' she says and bursts out laughing.

My body clenches suddenly, then goes cold. Is she going to start now too? Won't anyone just leave me in peace? This is how I look, everyone can just deal with it. What does she care about my curly hair? Or freckles or knobbly knees?

But she looks really cheerful. There is a sparkle in her sharp, icy eyes.

'Oh, come on,' she says. 'Come on, Vilma, I'm just kidding. It was a joke. I'd bloody love to have hair like yours!'

'Vinga,' I hiss. 'My name is Vinga.'

And then I stomp down to the water's edge.

'What the hell? Vinga, that's what I said. I know your name,' I heard her say from further up the beach.

I wade a little way into the water, take off my sailor's cap and throw it onto the pebbles. Pull up a bit of seaweed in my hands, the type that Grandpa says is actually called sea lace, put it on my head and let it drape down over my red curls.

Then I stomp back up to Ruth with saltwater running down my shoulders and I narrow my eyes at her.

'Vinga,' she says. 'Vinga, I knew that. Vinga, Vinga, Vinga. Nice name. Bit weird, but nice.'

Weird, weird, weird.

Then I see a smile spread slowly across her face again. Those little wrinkles around her eyes and that icy sparkle.

She backs up as I approach.

'Don't come near me like that. I hate the water, remember? No! Stay away from me.'

I threaten to come closer and she starts to run.

When Grandpa comes down with the picnic basket, this is how he finds us. Running, screaming, laughing.

'Stop it, stop it, stop it!'

Grandpa just walks over calmly to inspect the boat. He feels the newly bored holes. Runs his hand across the gunwale. Then he sits down by the rocks and sets out our snacks.

I don't know why but I feel sort of embarrassed when we come over to him. We're out of breath. Ruth is laughing so hard she has to sit down. My shirt is soaked. Grandpa offers Ruth a glass and looks at me.

'Sooo, you've found yourself some company down here.'

My heart, my heart, my heart. It's thumping, thumping, thumping.

'Well, she actually came from up there,' I say and point up to the lighthouse.

Then I realise I probably shouldn't tell him about her death-defying climb. That she could have died right then and there.

Grandpa looks at Ruth. A long, suspicious, questioning look. Then he tries to smooth down his wild eyebrows. It doesn't work.

'Sooo, are you an angel or something?'

We take our bikes to the shop. We have a basket each and Grandpa has those bags that go either side of the bike.

We cycle out past the sheep field and up towards the lighthouse. The sheep watch us dumbly as we pass, then they just carry on chewing, grinding their teeth like perpetual motion machines.

We swing past that little grove of trees that Grandpa calls the Great Wood, home to the only biggish trees on the island. Otherwise it's just bushes and brambles, bushes and brambles. On the other side of the road is Ylva's house, and when we cycle past we have to ring our bells and wave.

Grandpa leans forward over the handle bars like some proper pro cyclist. The tendons bulge in his neck and the straps of his bags flap in the wind.

Soon we come to that little cluster of houses they call a village. There is only one road with a few little white houses that sort of lean down towards the harbour, but we only go there to buy fish or crab. Or wave goodbye to someone. Like a mother.

We like crab, me and Grandpa. Mum is a vegetarian and Dad hates shellfish, but I'm like Grandpa. In the mornings we often say that we will head down to the harbour to see if the fishermen have brought in anything tasty.

But later, when afternoon comes, we decide we can get by just fine with eggs, potatoes and salad. And tomatoes. Rhubarb lemonade, currants; we've got everything right here.

'The potatoes are excellent this year,' says Grandpa. He says it every year.

A bell chimes when we enter the shop. It always smells cold in here and sometimes I point out things I think look pretty or tasty.

'Bah,' says Grandpa. I know what he means by that. Unnecessary luxuries.

Ruth's granny waddles over to us and holds out her arms. As usual. And as usual, she says how wonderful it is to see us. And that it seems we are joined at the hip. She always says this, but this time she grabs the peaks of our sailor's caps and bursts out laughing.

I can never tell if she's trying to be nice or if she's just mean.

I was afraid of her when I was little. I have no memory of Ruth, but she must have been here too. Back when Mum and I used to hang out on the swimming beach down by the village.

Whenever Grandpa and I are in the village everyone comes over to chat to us. They would like to see more of him, they think he keeps to himself at home too much, and it seems like they're too shy to visit him, unless it's for something super important. Maybe they all think he's *a bit weird*, like Ruth does.

Maybe it was her granny who said so to begin with.

Like everyone isn't a bit weird out here . . .

While Ruth's granny is talking to Grandpa, who barely responds except to nod and smile awkwardly, I amble through the little shop and look around. I think Ruth might be here, but there's no one but Grandpa and me.

There is one shelf I always come back to. It displays books about the island. Books with pictures from the past. You can see the lighthouse, Grandpa's house, the old boats.

49

I recognise the surnames and the old fishing boats. The same pebbles, same sea and same surnames; only the people are new.

And suddenly Grandpa is standing in front of me with bags in his hands. He is ready, he says. And he has ordered the rope end caps that we need, and that glue, or something like that, which he actually thinks is cheating but might be all right anyway.

Then he takes a book off the shelf. Dark blue with a gold anchor on the cover.

'You should have this,' he says and hurries back to the counter.

'Ring this up as well,' he calls to Ruth's granny and waves the book in the air.

Then we hurry home and hope that no one sees us.

We just give a quick wave to the old men on the bench outside the shop and try to look like we're in a rush.

When we get home we sit down outside on the front step. Grandpa lights his pipe and takes out his fancy pen. The one that needs to be filled with ink. The one he uses to write letters in English.

'Instead of the phone,' he says.

Sometimes he gets me to cycle down to the boats to deliver the letters. I read the addresses: Auckland, Halifax, Palermo . . .

Grandpa takes out the blue book to show me. I flick through it to see what could be so important. But it's blank.

Just white pages.

I was hoping for shipwrecks and great whales. Record-breaking fish and deserted islands. Storms and the angle of list around the Outer Hebrides.

I look questioningly at Grandpa. But he just yanks the book out of my hands and opens it up on the first page.

Then he writes in his swirly handwriting, right across the middle:

Logbook.

And in the top corner: *For my granddaughter, the Captain.* And then he signs and dates it.

Then he says that all proper boats need a logbook. I should use it to note the weather, wind and route.

'Well, you can write whatever you want, but always the weather, wind and direction of sail. Courses. Observations.'

I say thank you. Then he takes a few puffs on his pipe and gazes out to sea.

The sun is blazing.

Now I'm sitting here on the beach with my logbook. It's too hot to work on the boat. Grandpa was just here with egg sandwiches and lemonade. He lay down and snored for a bit in the sunshine, then woke up with a start.

'Right, there's things that want doing,' he said before disappearing back up the steps.

But I wouldn't be surprised if he has just lain down under the lilac bush and gone to sleep again. Nothing else to be done on a day like this, he likes to say.

OK, Grandpa said to note down the weather and wind.

Sunny, hot and no wind at all. And I don't have a course, because I'm not even sailing. Not yet.

I won't get to any foreign harbours in this weather. So I just sit here staring at the white pages with no idea what to write. White as sunshine on the sea's surface. The pages, my thoughts. Blank. I've never had a diary. Dad has given me various notebooks in an effort to get me writing.

'You're so good at it,' he said. I've no idea why. 'You've got such an imagination. Write whatever you want. Poems, journal entries, good quotes you come across.'

'*Carpe diem*,' I retorted irritably. Then the book ended up in a pile by my bed and I probably watched some crappy TV show instead.

Nope, I take notes in my head. And they're turning into full-blown daydreams now. I've written things on my mobile a couple of times. Like on the tram when I'm all invisible and can listen to everyone else's conversations and dream away. I invent complex stories about every single person in the carriage.

But a diary? Does anything happen to me that's exciting enough to write down?

I put pen to paper and watch the blue ink slowly spread across the whiteness.

'What are you writing that's so secret then?'

Ruth is standing beside me. How does she keep sneaking up on me like this? How can she walk across pebbles without making a sound?

I snap the book shut suspiciously quickly and toss it in the boat.

She flops down beside me in the shade, and there they are – the sparks – spreading through my body like fire. I feel shaky and anxious, but happy all the same.

'Damn, it's hot,' she says and looks like she's suffering.

My mouth feels dry and I trip over my words but manage to mumble:

'So . . . go for a . . . swim then.'

I hear how harsh it sounds.

'I hate the sea.'

'Oh yeah, of course.'

Then we say nothing for a bit. We look at the sea and quivering heat. My head is spinning with all the things I should say, but nothing comes out.

'God, it's so fucking boring here. I just wanna go home. Everyone else is having super fun summers. Road trips in Europe and beach holidays in Greece.'

'Oh yeah, that would be perfect for you,' I say and manage to squeeze out an awkward chuckle. 'Seeing as you hate the sea and heat.'

'Yeah but,' she says, 'it's different in the Mediterranean. Anyway,' she continues, 'anyway most people are at home in the city. Just think of all the things you can get up to when you're free all day and can stay out as long as you want. Just think how much fun they're having now. Without me.'

I really do think about it and try to understand. But I literally can't think of a single fun thing to do in the city. And no one tells me how late I can stay out any more. I'm always home anyway.

'Oh, you don't get it,' she said. 'You're a total loser.'

I just nod. And everything goes grey again.

And I think back to spring in the city. Outside the classroom windows I could occasionally hear the sea. If I really concentrated I could hear a whisper of it from the other side of the grassy hill. I saw the bright, hazy sky with its thin veil of clouds and the tall grass swaying in the sea breeze. I saw the path winding down towards the beach through sand dunes, and sometimes I could even smell it.

Except there was no sea.

But there were times when, for just a brief moment, I *knew* it was there.

When I came out of school I couldn't bring myself to look, because I knew it would just be cycle paths and rose-hip bushes and the grassy hill sloping down to the city and all that grey.

I get up suddenly and then I'm standing there above her and looking at her twiggy legs and baggy black shirt.

Her hair is hanging in her face.

'God, you really don't get it, do you? I don't *want* to go to the city because I haven't got any friends there. And my dad has, like, disappeared and my mum just lies on the sofa crying and watching TV, or she goes totally nuts and pretends everything is so fucking great, and here I've got my grandpa who doesn't talk shit at me, and here I've got my boat to work on and I don't have to think about all that other stuff . . .'

She looks at me with wide eyes. Shocked that I talked back, that I could get angry.

My heart is hammering and heat is spreading up my neck and into my cheeks. I just turn around and go. I fix my sights on the steps and march towards them with decisive strides, like in the movies.

Fuck Ruth. I don't give a damn about her cool friends and mysterious hat. What do I care about her elegant eyebrows and straight hair? I couldn't care less about her boring summer. Her stupid whingeing.

I realise I'm crying and feel a hand on my shoulder. As usual, I didn't hear her bare footsteps on the beach. I turn around, making no effort to hide my tears.

'Sorry,' she says, looking down at the ground. 'Sorry, I'm a total idiot.'

And then we sit next to each other again. In the shade of the boat. And, obviously, I end up feeling bad for her. I end up making the effort.

'At least you can climb,' I suggest.

'Too hot,' she says.

'Read then.'

'That's the only thing I do! When I'm not in the shop.'

'Learn to play the accordion.'

'Ha!'

55

Then I pluck up the courage to ask.

'OK. Help me do up the boat?' I say, expecting an outburst.

She looks at me for a long time, then says:

'Are you sure?'

I just shrug.

'OK,' she says and stands up. 'Tell me what to do.'

And then I show her what I've done and what's left to do and I teach her the names of the tools and all the parts of the boat. And then suddenly there she is with a hammer and dowels, having a go.

'But hey,' she says. 'Remember: I still hate boats.'

Now we meet on the beach practically every day.

The listless birds fly a few metres away when we come. Then they just hang out staring at us while we work on the boat. They've become like friends. One gull has even started coming up to us and we feed it bits of egg sandwich. After the first time it occurred to us that it might be a bit wrong to feed egg to birds. But it didn't want anything else. It wanted egg sandwich.

Sometimes the gull sits up on the fore of the boat while we work. It tilts its head to one side and watches us. We call it the Sand Witch. Because its singing is so ugly. Well, I say singing, it's more of a squawk that sounds like an evil cackle. And it likes sandwiches.

The boat has turned white with bird poo but that can't be helped. I can wash it off later. Or not.

We sweat in the sun and I have to go down to the sea from time to time to dunk my hair and hat. Ruth looks at me in disgust when I do that. She stays in the shade of her black hat.

Grandpa comes down to check on us now and then.

He doesn't say much when Ruth is with me, but he looks at the boat and tells me what to do next. He often nods and hums in that way of his.

And I think he is glad that I have company.

Ruth doesn't do much. She mainly sits on the gunwale asking questions and telling stories. Talking about *the gang*. She has one of those, she says. They're always hanging out together and getting up to all sorts. She got with one of the boys before, but says she's never really been in love.

'Have you?' she says.

I freeze.

'Have I what?'

'Been in love, of course.'

'Dunno,' I say simply.

'What do you mean you don't know?'

She can be pretty pushy sometimes. Doesn't know how to keep her mouth shut. That's what Grandpa says about most people. That they don't know how to keep their mouths shut.

'You and I know how, at least,' I always say back to him.

Then we'll just sit in silence until I can't hold it in any more and burst out laughing.

'I think you'd *know* if you'd been in love,' says Ruth, as if it's totally obvious and I'm a complete idiot.

She kicks at the pebbles. Looks around for pretty shells.

'It's a really unique feeling, and you just know,' she says and looks at me questioningly.

I just carry on with what I'm doing and wonder how she knows. And I practise keeping my mouth shut. I'm usually pretty good at it. I usually like it too.

Still, I miss Ruth and miss talking to her on those days when she has to help in the shop, when deliveries need unpacking and pricing and putting out in the right places on the shelves. Jars of marmalade and fishing lures.

Sometimes I think it's nice to be alone, but then it occurs to me that I almost feel lonely.

But I can always talk to the Sand Witch.

Sometimes I feel like it understands.

One evening Ylva comes running from the sheep field. Grandpa and I are sitting in the shade of the lilac bush. He is naming birds. The occasional chirp comes from the Great Wood and he tells me what bird it is. I sit with a bird guide, look up each name and study the pictures. Icterine warbler, Eurasian blackcap, scarlet rosefinch . . .

We drink rhubarb lemonade, as usual. There is plenty.

I see Grandpa sort of flinch when he sees Ylva. It's very strange to see her in such a hurry. It must be something important. Then I hear that she's not calling to him but to me:

'Vinga, Vinga! Your mum called.'

And my chest tightens and my heart flutters and I become a mess. I look at Grandpa and can tell that he is making an effort to appear calm. But there is worry in his eyes.

He tries to reply like it's no big deal.

'Probably best we go and talk to her,' he says. Like *we* don't always call *her*. Like Mum has ever called us before.

We follow Ylva to her house and I try to think of something else. Don't start imagining what Mum might say. Don't think about what might have happened. Don't think about Mum's weepy eyes and runny nose.

Grandpa's strides are longer and quicker than usual.

He and Ylva don't say a word. Like they're zipped and buttoned up. We're walking faster than ever but the journey feels very long.

When we come into Ylva's kitchen there is a faint smell of burning. There always is. It kind of smells like a carpentry workshop. Ylva says she'll put on some coffee and Grandpa says it's probably best if he begins the conversation, he'll call and talk to Mum first. But I walk straight past him and into the next room. Sit on the little stool, slam the door shut with my foot, and pick up the phone.

'Vinga, hi.'

'Mum.'

'Oh my love, how are you?'

'Fine. I'm fine. What is it?'

'What are you getting up to?'

'I'm fixing up my boat, of course. But what is it? Why are you calling? Has something happened?'

'Happened? No . . .'

'Tell me!'

'What? I just called to talk to you. I miss you, you know.'

'And that's all?'

'Yes and . . . I just really miss you a lot. I need to hear your voice sometimes.'

I hear her laughing from across the sea. Then the ice melts inside me. All at once. I start shaking and suddenly I'm sitting there with the phone in my hand and sobbing. I wipe my nose with my hand, but it's too late. She's heard me.

'My little girl . . . are you OK? Are you crying?'

And then I can't talk any more. Tears flow. Snot runs. It's hard to breathe. I make some weird sounds.

'Aw, darling, what is it? I thought you were having such a good time out there on the island. Is something wrong? Do you miss home? I'll come and get you, OK? Sweetheart?'

I try to speak. To defend myself. I don't want to cry, but I can't help it. If she hadn't called everything would have been normal and I wouldn't be sitting here crying, in desperate need of a hug. Doesn't she get that? I'm fine, as long as I can get away from the stupid mainland.

'Mm,' is all I can squeeze out.

Then suddenly I feel angry. Angry at Mum with her 'darling' and 'aw' and 'little girl'. I'm not a fucking little girl! Angry at that whole world, still there, just a couple of hours' boat ride away.

The door opens with a bang and in storms Grandpa. With his white hair sticking out all over the place and his eyes all serious. His whole body is tight and tensed.

He snatches the phone from my hand and practically shouts to Mum, who is so far away.

'What's happened?'

On our way home from Ylva's, the sun is setting over the sea. I wish I was up in my usual spot on the cliff. I want to be alone. It feels like I haven't got all my tears out yet. But Grandpa is walking beside me, talking and laughing. He is walking normally again, slowly. Now and then he stops to listen out for something.

I can't hear a thing. Not even the sea.

Grandpa says that can happen sometimes. If you're feeling anxious about something.

And he says it's just that Mum misses me, which is understandable. So does Dad. And he says that Mum told him that she's actually doing a lot better, even though she feels sad sometimes. And she and Dad are discussing this and that and are doing their best to sort things out.

This and that, this and that.

He says that everything should be more or less like it was by the time I go home.

'Except not really,' I say in a baby voice.

He gets it and laughs.

Grandpa says that we should stop worrying, that this is the hottest summer in a long time and we should do all we can to get that boat on the water pronto. He says that I'll go back from the island in autumn having learned to sail, and everything else will have sorted itself out. And it's about time I finally beat him at chess.

It's hard not to think about Mum and Dad and the city and all that. Mum said on the phone that she thinks about me all the time and wonders how we're doing out here. That was after

Grandpa had finished talking to her. I wanted to say a proper goodbye, and let her know everything is OK.

'I've made a friend as well,' I said, trying to make it sound like the most normal thing in the world. Absolutely no big deal.

But I just *knew* she would overreact.

'Oh wow, that makes me so happy!' she said and tried to push me to tell her more.

She got a name out of me: Ruth. And hair colour: jet black. That was it.

'Mum, give me a break,' I said. 'That's enough. And I'm not a bloody sweetheart.'

Before we hung up she said all that same stuff about how she thinks about me all the time and I had to promise to call every other evening, or every third evening max. And she should only call in case of emergency. She can't make us worry like that.

'Good,' Grandpa says on the way home. Then he says he hadn't realised so many days had passed since we last called, and I say the same thing.

'I'm not used to talking much in general,' he says. 'And you've been busy.'

Which is just as it should be, Grandpa says, and I agree.

When we get home that evening we hang our sailor's caps up on their hooks as usual. Then we sit at the table as usual. Grandpa puts water on the stove to boil for tea and lights his pipe. He has two stiff drinks tonight, because he needs it. But he doesn't get out the cards. Or the dice, or the chess set. He says he's going to tell me a story.

A story about fathers.

'It was one of those early spring days,' he begins.

'It was one of those early spring days. A clear day when the birds are flying north. Songs and squawks on the ice sheets. White-tailed eagles were perched far out on the ice floe, staring.

'On that day three men set out across the ice. Straight towards the low sun, they walked. They dragged behind them a black, tarred sailing boat and carried rifles. Bird hunters, they were, out to shoot some oldsquaws, eiders and goldeneyes. In the boat they had their packed lunch and boots and space for their catch.

'They moved out slowly until they heard the beat of wings. The boat was easily dragged across the ice. Then they stopped there and their gunshots could be heard from land.

'Bird hunters, they were. Fathers, they were.

'They had left their families behind with promises of a great catch. One of their children had begged to be allowed to join them. He wanted so badly to see all the birds. He wanted to hear the gunshots. But he was told no.

'All day the little boy awaited his father's return. He stood down on the shore, whence the hunters had set out. He sat on a rock and stared. He paced up and down the beach.

'He was freezing cold.

'He got up and found a bothy to lean on. The sun shone and he was able to keep warm there. He stared out across the ice, but he couldn't see them any more, the fathers. The bird hunters. All day he waited down there by the shore. He stayed until it got dark and mothers and siblings came down worrying and wondering.

'Out on the ice, the bird hunters had already got a few oldsquaws in their boat. Focused, they aimed their rifles at a group of eiders.

'The ice groaned and sang and they noticed the crack too late.

'"Goddammit!" they cried, but their boat was too far away.

'A black grave opened up between them and the boat. One of the fathers prepared to jump, but the crack quickly grew and became too wide.

'A moment's hesitation was all it took.

'Hesitation for fear of the cold, dark water. For hope that it would turn out all right.

'They were left stranded on that ice floe, watching as the black, tarred boat floated away from them, shining in the sun. Or perhaps they floated away from it. What happened next, we can only guess. And never know for sure.

'Never again would that little boy on the beach see his father. Nor the other children theirs. And the wives who stood there with their children hugging their legs would never see their husbands.

'And many years later that little boy would search the length of the island's shores for something. For traces of his father. But nothing. And he would think about that cold, black sea and the fish in there and what happens to a big, strong father down at the bottom. He would have trouble sleeping. He would wake up and scream. He would miss him.

'And he would remain for ever by the sea.'

Our tea is finished and Grandpa gets up and stretches. He says he's going 'out for a piss'.

'I often think of that day still,' he says as he walks to the door.

He opens the door, turns around and looks at me.

'And I'm ever grateful that my father didn't let me go out on the ice with him. And you should be too.'

Then he closes the door and I'm left sitting here alone.

And there's my heart, in the right place.

I feel it beating; I am alive.

I was born and I exist. And the sea . . .

'There, you see,' says Ruth.

'See what?'

'The sea is evil. Lethal. Watch out, sailor.'

We sit in the shade of the sailing boat sipping Grandpa's rhubarb lemonade. I just told her about Grandpa's father. The story of how he went missing. I haven't been able to think about anything else. And I don't really understand why he told me. He is always telling me I shouldn't worry about my dad. Still, I feel a sense of calm inside. That everything is going to be OK. Or that it doesn't matter.

'I wonder what became of the fathers down there,' I say, because I've been thinking about it non-stop. Gruesome figures with swirling hair and dead, staring eyes.

'Huh?'

'I mean, down under the sea. Once they've sunk to the bottom. Like, what happens to them then?'

'They become fish food, I guess,' says Ruth.

Then we stare into space for a bit.

'And it's not only fathers,' she says after a while. 'Anyone can drown. That's what happens out here. It happens all the time, people just disappear. Fathers and other people too.'

She says she has heard loads of stories about the dangers of the sea. About children going missing, boats sinking, corpses eaten by fish. I keep my eyes fixed on the calm blue and think about its depths. About everything that's down there. And everything that isn't. The emptiness. The vast emptiness.

'It terrifies me,' says Ruth, looking down at the pebbles.

'It makes me feel calm,' I say. 'The sea and all that unknown.'

I tell her that whenever I have nightmares, the sea comes to my rescue. Suddenly the open water is there and I can jump in and swim away from whatever danger was chasing me.

'Did you know . . .' I add. 'Did you know that ninety-five per cent of the world's oceans are unexplored?'

She just gives me a look. As if she would care.

But she says: 'Cool.' So I carry on.

'Yeah, so that means there's bound to be loads of creatures down there that humans have never discovered. Animals and plants that live in a whole different world. Have you heard of giant squid?'

'You've got cute freckles,' she says, running her fingers over my spotted shin.

It sends a shiver all through my body and feels weird and I flinch and pull my leg away. It is pure reflex. It immediately seems pointless and silly.

'Sorry,' she says.

I just swallow and carry on.

'Anyway, so no one knew anything about giant squid, but there were stories about them, rumours of ships being pulled underwater and stuff, and then they discovered . . .'

'Freckles, aren't they also little sea creatures?'

'Cockles.'

'Mm?'

'Aren't you thinking of cockles?'

'Oh,' she says and laughs. She gives me a nudge and her laughter doesn't sound mean. She looks happy.

'Cockles,' I say again and feel laughter bubbling up inside

me too and soon we're both sitting on the pebbles laughing in the face of the calm sea.

I'm not even sure why it's so funny, but the laughter just keeps coming. The birds don't seem to care. Everything is normal, except we're just killing ourselves laughing.

'I hate cockles,' she says, still laughing. 'I. Hate. Cockles . . .'

Then, once the laughter has reduced to little giggles, she says it again, that she hates cockles. She looks down.

'But I like your freckles.'

Then I extend my legs again, so they're lying straight across the pebbles. It burns the back of my thighs and calves; the pebbles are sharp and burning, but I can take it.

'I used to hate them,' I say, looking at my legs.

My freckles are like islands in an archipelago. In some places they fuse into a large landmass, tricky to navigate, lots of hidden rocks.

'I hate my freckles and my hair and these lips.'

I pout to make my lips extra big. I don't know why.

She smiles.

'They're fine,' she says and laughs. 'What about me? Pale and bony. Like a skeleton.'

I say nothing. Just smile. I remember the first time she appeared on the beach; I did think she looked kind of creepy.

'I am death . . .'

I say it in a dark, drawling voice, but she doesn't get my movie reference.

'You're weird,' is all she says. 'Why don't you tell me more about those giant jellyfish?'

'Squid?'

'Whatever.'

'You really want to know?'

'Sure, go on.'

'Well, dead squid started washing up on beaches. In Norway, Japan, Australia . . . Huge, they were, like ten, fifteen metres . . .'

'Hey, check this out,' Ruth calls suddenly and starts digging among the pebbles. She picks out a mussel shell that's all round and stripy. Grey and pink with deep, even grooves.

'Pretty,' I say. 'A scallop.'

I know it is. Grandpa told me. He would always walk around pointing at things and teaching me about them when I was little. It was like he had named them all himself: turnstone, starfish, limestone . . .

'Oh,' says Ruth. 'It's not alive, it's just a shell.'

And then she splits it right at the hinge into two identical pieces, like two little plates. She puts one in the pocket of her long black shirt. She gives the other one to me.

'You should have this,' she says. 'For good luck at sea.'

Then she gets up and starts walking away.

'Gotta help Granny,' she says and waves goodbye in that way of hers.

Soon she is just a little black speck.

I stay sitting in the shade, fingering the scallop shell. Then I put it in my pocket. And for the rest of the day I go around with one hand in my pocket and feel the ridges, the smoothness.

Later, when I'm working with a screwdriver, I have to stop from time to time and stick my hand in my pocket. Just touch it a bit.

I saw a documentary once about a Japanese scientist who dedicated his whole life to the search for a living giant squid. To this day he is the only person who managed to photograph one, it was like a flash of lightning deep in the sea.

I remember I was sitting on the sofa, and Dad was probably working at his desk and Mum was in the kitchen, and I remember the exact feeling in my belly.

Like now, every time I run my thumb over this shell . . . definitely from some sort of scallop.

A quick, clear flash deep down in the darkness.

The next time I see Ruth is in the shop. We've run out of butter and a couple of other things and I don't mind cycling down.

I am standing in the dairy section when the little door in the corner opens and I see Ruth come in and walk over to one of the shelves. She is rooting around among the jars when I come over. I have one hand in my pocket, stroking the smooth inside of the shell with my thumb.

'Hey.' I try to say it like she usually does, but it comes out wrong. She notices too. She lets out a little laugh as she takes a jar of marmalade off the shelf.

'Breakfast. She can't see me,' she whispers and nods to indicate her granny at the counter.

'Will I see you later?' I ask softly. It feels secret somehow.

'I'll try to sneak away,' Ruth whispers and glances over.

Then she creeps back to the door in the corner. The door that leads into the house. Ruth's world. She does a little wave with the marmalade jar and shuts the door quietly and carefully.

Then I stand at the counter while her granny rings up my shopping and packs it for me. The way she smiles at me feels very fake. I'm having trouble seeing her as anything other than a prison guard.

My thumb is almost starting to chafe in my pocket.

I have a song stuck in my head as I sit up here on the cliff. The sun is setting and the birds are flapping around and shrieking down below. Seagulls probably. So annoying.

They do this every evening. Swoop, fly around, scream and fight over territory. Soon they'll settle down to sleep, I suppose.

But sometimes one of them just, like, soars across the sea and into the sunset. Far out, further and further. I don't understand where it's going.

And this song keeps going round and round my head:

Out on the open sea, out on the open sea . . .

It was Dad who played it to me one afternoon in the kitchen back home. He said it made him think of me when he heard it. He would do that sometimes. Come home with some song he just *had* to play me, or some book that he just *had* to buy me. And he wanted so badly for me to love it.

'Listen,' he'd say eagerly. 'Listen, Vinga, please, you're going to love this.'

Or: 'You absolutely have to read this. You just have to.'

'OK,' I'd say and the new book would end up in the pile by my bed.

I intended to read them, I really did, but Dad would ask about them and start nagging and then they lost their appeal.

So they just sat there in that pile.

I should read poetry, he said, it would suit me. He, like my teacher, figured I must be artistic just because I have wild hair and wear colourful clothes. A poet is the best thing a person can be, according to Dad. Probably according to my teacher too. And poets are probably a bit introverted, like me. His name was Janne, my teacher. Talk about an unpoetic name. Ruth is better. Vinga isn't bad either. Angelica is the worst.

And I said I wanted to be a sailor. Poetry seemed hard to understand.

'The singer looks like you,' said Dad, next to the speaker in the kitchen.

He googled her and held up his phone. Well, she had big hair, not bright red, auburn maybe. And plump lips, a baggy shirt. She looked really cool, and I guess Dad thought so too.

We didn't look much alike.

'A bit like Bob Dylan,' he said, still looking at the woman.

'I don't like Bob Dylan,' I said.

'Yeah Vinga, I know, but just listen to this. Listen!'

And I listened. I must have listened to that song ten times in a row. Sitting there on the kitchen counter while Dad was getting on with other things.

When the apocalypse comes
the sun will be drawn
will be drawn

'What are you singing?'

It's Ruth, of course. Always appearing out of nowhere. Suddenly there she is, standing on the cliff. Where I've always been alone. Wanted to be alone. Still, they come: the fire sparks.

She sits down next to me. Close. An intense heat seems to radiate from her, though you wouldn't think it to look at her. I can feel my heart through my skin and bones. Fluttering like an aspen leaf.

'What was it? It sounded good.'

She sounds unusually cheerful.

'Just a song. "The Eel", it's called.'

Then I just start talking. I don't know why this always happens with Ruth. That I always start babbling away, even though I usually prefer silence and barely respond when spoken to. I remember Dad used to say that when I was little.

'You could at least respond when spoken to,' he'd say with a frown.

But I couldn't. Words didn't come out. And it only got worse the more he pressed.

I don't know why, I guess it's just the way I am. But with Ruth it's like the opposite is happening. I can't stop talking. I just stare out to sea and talk.

I talk about eels. About the secrets of those mysterious, snaking fish. I tell her about how they leave their homes and cross oceans to get to the Sargasso Sea to mate. That's the only place where scientists have found eel spawn. Nowhere else. No one knows how they get there. How they know where to go or how their young grow up and spread all over the world and can be found in dark, muddy lakes.

I stare at the horizon and the slowly sinking sun.

'So where is that sea?' she asks from next to me.

I can feel her eyes on me, but don't dare look.

'The Atlantic,' I say. 'Like, the Bahamas.'

'Wow, awesome,' she says.

I laugh.

'There was an eel that lived in a well in Skåne for a hundred and fifty years,' I say. 'That one never got there.'

'Got where?'

'To the Sargasso Sea, of course. The Bahamas. Though I guess it must have been born there. It must have felt such a strong pull towards the Sargasso Sea while it swam round and round and round its little well for a hundred and fifty years without getting anywhere. Imagine.'

'You know so much,' she says.

'No one knows much about eels, that's the point.'

'I didn't even know that,' she says.

'They can wriggle over land when they're heading for the ocean, slithering like snakes. The eels, that is.'

'Ugh, gross.'

Then she starts moving and fiddling with something next to me. Rustling something and I have to turn to look at her. That pale, pointed face. That black, glossy hair.

'What are you doing?' I ask when I see that she has a cigarette packet in her hand. And a lighter with the price sticker still on.

'Nicked them from the shop,' she says. 'Ever tried it?'

My stomach clenches again, but this time it feels horrible.

'It could start a fire,' I say, thinking of all those warnings on the radio.

But I just feel stupid as soon as I've said it. When she offers me one, I shake my head. She sighs. I know, I'm so 'fucking boring', but I really don't want to.

She lights it, takes a puff and shuts her eyes. I glare at her. The smoke rises in a straight line. Like an eel.

Then she starts coughing. She lies down in the dry, yellow grass and coughs. The gulls are quiet now. The only sound is Ruth. First coughing and then, when a sheep bleats somewhere behind us, laughter.

'Meh,' comes out between peals of laughter.

I watch her sort of drag the cigarette along the dusty earth to put it out. My stomach relaxes, which feels great. Calm again, I lie down next to her.

'You stink,' I say. It smells nothing like the sweet, smooth smoke from Grandpa's pipe.

'Sorry,' she says. 'It wasn't really like I imagined it would be.'

Then we lie there and she tells me again about everything she misses in the city. That she feels like a prisoner here on the island and that her granny is really a tough-nut prison guard. That she thought a cigarette would feel like freedom, but it didn't really work.

I smile up at the sky where the stars are slowly coming out.

'Now the angels are lighting their cigars,' I say.

That's what Grandpa always says when we look up at those glowing pin pricks.

'You're so weird,' she says. Which is fine by me.

Then everything is so silent. The sky so dark blue. By the time we get up to leave I realise I've missed the shipping forecast, tea and biscuits.

I wonder if Grandpa has gone to bed. If he is wondering where I am. I brush the dry grass and dust off Ruth's back. She picks something out of my hair.

'Thank god you're here at least,' she says before turning around and whisking herself away down to the village.

It takes some time to find the cigarette butt. I put it in my pocket and head for home.

It's a very peculiar feeling. That someone likes me. Someone apart from Mum or Grandpa. Or Dad. It's probably just for the summer. I'm sure everything will go back to how it was before when I go back home.

But still . . .

When Ruth and I walk and talk on the beach, or when we sit together in silence, or sand and scrape the boat, it feels like something special. Like the giant squid is there, something hidden and secret, flashing and glowing inside my body.

When we work on the boat it is mainly Ruth talking and me listening. Sometimes she gets annoyed if I don't answer. It's because my mind is somewhere else entirely and I have to try to pretend I've been listening. She easily gets annoyed over nothing and she complains a lot. But I just laugh at her and then she's all right again.

I tell Ruth things I've never told anyone before. They might not be secrets exactly, but personal things. I just haven't had anyone to tell before. Now they pour out of me.

I tell her about the cat Grandpa had one summer when I was little. It was supposed to be mine, but Mum named him Bengt. I loved that cat so much at first, before it started bringing home dead, or almost dead, little birds. I tell her how Grandpa would say what kind of birds they were, sigh and scratch his head, while I screamed at the cat and called it a monster. Every evening before I came through the door I'd ask Grandpa: How many murders today?

I tell her how happy Grandpa had sounded when, late one autumn, he called us in the city and told us Bengt was gone.

Taken by an eagle owl, Grandpa said. He sounded relieved and happy.

Mum said it served that monster of a cat right. I was horrified, even though I basically hated Bengt by then.

'You know he probably killed the cat himself, right?' says Ruth, but she can't know that. Eagle owls really can take cats and Bengt was so small. I don't want to know.

I tell her about the picture of a dead albatross I saw in the newspaper. Scientists had studied it and opened up its stomach. The contents were spread out around the bird corpse: lighters, balloons, plastic corks, bits of toys, Lego, shopping bags, plastic. Plastic, plastic, plastic . . .

'Seagulls are stupid,' Ruth replies, looking up at the cliff and the birds there.

'Albatross . . .' I say warily.

And she says: 'Whatever.'

It occurs to me that this is exactly how the kids in my class at school would respond. Then they'd carry on staring at their phones, utterly uninterested. And I would think they were idiots, those so-called classmates. But when Ruth says it I just laugh. I don't really know why, but it's actually funny.

I would never dream of telling anyone else these things.

I tell her about Mum and her mood swings, about Dad and his scarf and its smell, about Angelica and how she fusses and babies me. I do an impression of her, her swaying walk and dangling earrings.

Then Ruth laughs so hard she cries, then she strokes my back and tells me she understands.

'God, sounds tough,' she says.

Then we talk about something else. And it feels like we're the only two people in the world, and if this little island really were the whole world, just for these few weeks of summer, it would be enough. Just me and her. And the birds and stones and sea. No mainland, no disposable barbecues and forest fires. No babies growing in bellies. Everything would be simple.

And I'm not scared of making a fool of myself any more. I don't worry about what she thinks any more. I am me, and she can take me as I am.

One time she even said she wished she had the guts to dress like I do.

I didn't return the compliment. I was just really happy, though I'm not sure I totally believed her.

I figured she was probably just trying to make me feel good, like Dad used to.

But I have another feeling too, something like disappointment. This is my absolute best life. The pebble beach, the boat, the birds, Grandpa. But she keeps hinting that all this isn't good enough for her. *I'm* not really good enough for her. I often think she is only spending time with me because there's no one else. If her *gang* was here, hanging out in the village and the Great Wood and laughing together in the pub on Wednesday evenings, I would be all alone.

All alone again.

Ruth often talks about the city and her friends there, and how much she misses it. And I hate that gang of hers. I can picture them now: cool, fun, pretty, a pain in the butt . . .

Here, I'm all she has. Anxiety gnaws at me from deep inside.

82

Why does she want to hang out with me?
Sometimes a weird fringe-finned fish will just have to do.
Things would be so much easier if we'd never met.
Things would be so much more boring if we'd never met.

The Whale

Even from up here, on the steps down to the beach, I can hear that something's not right. It's the birds. They sound upset. Angry.

I hurry down and see a large cloud of white birds beyond the boat.

The sea is a mirror and the sun is blazing, as usual, and drift seaweed is glittering. But the rocks by the boat are still in shade.

I run down towards the bird-cloud and as I approach I see that black figure coming from the other direction. She is like a scarecrow.

When the gulls and terns see her they take off as one, fly up to the cliff, land, sit and wait, their eyes fixed on the thing lying on the beach. The black, glossy thing.

Ruth gets there first.

'What is it?' I ask.

'A seal,' she says. 'Dead.'

It is dead. But it looks more like a dolphin. It glistens in the sun and there is something like a shark fin on its back. Pointed nose. Its eyes are closed and it's perfectly still. It doesn't seem to be breathing.

I, on the other hand, am more alive than I've been in a long time. Pounding heart and heavy breaths. I look up at Ruth. She is crying.

I walk around the dead body, whatever it is, and stand next to her. Put my arm around her and she flinches slightly before throwing her arms around me and hugging me back. Hard.

'Oh,' is all she says. And: 'God.'

I stroke her back. It feels good. Feels right somehow. Her hug makes me feel all warm. Although she is bony, she feels soft and warm. Then it's like the warmth spreads all over my body. We stand there for a long time. She smells good, like pencils. She leans her head on my shoulder. I feel her whole body in mine, like an imprint.

But eventually she lets go. And I feel empty.

She wipes her eyes on her shirt sleeve, and says 'Oh god' again and I wonder what she means.

Eventually I tell her we have to go and get Grandpa. He'll know what animal it is. He'll know what to do. Surely someone will have to come and deal with it.

Ruth nods gently. I ask her if she wants to come with me, but she says she'll stay.

I give her a little wave, tell her I'll be back soon, and run to the steps.

'A porpoise,' says Grandpa.

He knows. He says it's a type of whale.

I look at him.

'A whale? That little thing? It looks more like a dolphin.'

'Dolphins are whales too,' he says simply, as if he were the one who decides such things.

Then he puts his hand on my shoulder in that way he does sometimes.

'It's been years since I saw a porpoise. That's some discovery you've made.'

He says there was probably something wrong with it, that it was sick. Otherwise it wouldn't have navigated so poorly. It must have got stranded yesterday evening and then lain there all night and died. Because it's been a little while now since it took its last breath,' he says.

But my attention is elsewhere. Looking around, searching the beach.

Ruth has vanished. I was sure she would wait here until I came back with Grandpa, but she's nowhere to be seen. I've almost forgotten about the porpoise. I think only of her.

But Grandpa is in a flap. Jabbering away more than ever. Telling me about the time he saw orca whales. Talking about a book called *Moby Dick*. I have to read it, he says, but I don't want book recommendations, even from him. And then he tells me everything he knows about porpoises, and he points at its head and shows me its blow hole. He tells me he's seen a dolphin here before, just below the lighthouse, and wild boar, and a bit further south a dead minke whale washed up on the beach once.

Then he has to hurry up to Ylva's house to make a phone call. To the Natural History Museum so they can send out a marine biologist, because they want to be informed of dead seals and whales so they can take samples and run tests.

This evening, sitting up here on the cliff, I'm not really thinking about the porpoise. I'm just wondering where Ruth went. I wonder what her 'Oh god' meant, and I wonder why I can't just get the words out that I want to say.

Back at the house I drink my tea quickly, roll the dice reluctantly. And Grandpa can tell something is wrong. But he's excited, if that word can really apply to him, and keeps talking about the porpoise and what the people at the museum said. I respond briefly and go to bed before the shipping forecast.

'It's OK,' says Grandpa. 'I'll listen to it alone.'

And as I'm lying in my bed and trying to sleep I can still feel the imprint of Ruth's body against mine.

That's how I fall asleep.

But as I'm drifting off I hear the radio from the kitchen: high pressure continues, gentle winds, no rainfall.

And the forests continue to burn inland.

They've had to call in firefighters from Poland and Italy now.

After that, working undisturbed on the boat becomes impossible.

We are just on our way out, Grandpa and me. We have put on our sailor's caps and I haven't bothered with the sun cream that Mum packed for me and is always going on about.

'You know what sensitive skin you have,' she says.

And 'sweetheart' again.

Grandpa says it's fine not to wear sun cream, that a sailor ought to be a little ruddy faced.

We stand on the front step and stretch. The sheep look up at us curiously, their jaws grinding away.

Then a man comes walking towards us with a huge bag over his shoulder. He looks kind of weird. With long boots, a hat and big sunglasses. Loaded with gadgets. Bulging pockets everywhere.

'Now that,' Grandpa whispers to me, '*that* is a marine biologist. A peculiar breed.'

Then he comes over and introduces himself, the marine biologist. He points and waves and complains at how out of the way we live.

Grandpa just laughs at him – he actually sounds a bit unkind. Anyway, we go down to the beach and more and more people keep arriving. They've all heard about the discovery of the porpoise. Everybody wants to talk to me.

There are people all over the beach and some of them want to look at my sailing boat and praise me and give me advice.

'Keep scraping,' they say and laugh.

'Here you need one of those fittings, oh what's it called . . .'

'Don't you have a trolley to transport it?'

At times I feel very small among all the people.

Then all of a sudden there she is with a notebook and camera, the journalist, saying she wants a little chat with me, because I'm the one who found the whale.

'There are whales and there are whales,' I say. 'Some are much bigger.'

Grandpa straightens my sailor's cap before I have my picture taken and I let him. The journalist asks questions and I answer briefly and quietly. I just want this to be over, for things to go back to normal.

Then the marine biologist comes over, says I've done well, I did all the right things.

'Thank you,' he says.

Even though I didn't do anything. I just stood there next to the porpoise with someone else's hair in my mouth and felt the warmth of someone else's body.

That's all.

When I wake up, Grandpa isn't home. He is always the first thing I see when I peek out from behind the curtain, but today he's not there. No cup on the table. No fire in the wood stove. No coffee pot, no crossword.

But the radio is on. So he has heard the first shipping forecast.

I call out, pathetically:

'Grandpa, Grandpa?'

Though I know he won't answer.

His hat isn't hanging on the hook and his boots are gone. My body turns to ice. My heart, which has been in the right place practically all summer, jolts and lands wrong. Something must have happened.

Something must have happened at home. In the city. Summer is over.

And then I just stand there, in the hall at the bottom of the stairs to the loft. I haven't frozen like this since last spring. It happened a few times back then. I would be standing somewhere and just sort of get stuck. Like I disappeared for a few seconds, minutes even, I don't know. Mum shouted at me to snap out of it, that I was frightening her, but I didn't hear her. She shook me until I woke up and felt dizzy and had to go and lie down. And then came the tears.

After it had happened a few times Mum came into my room and said we needed to have a talk. And after we'd had a talk she said that I needed to talk. And when I replied that we had literally just talked, she said I had to talk to someone else. A school councillor or psychiatrist.

But it was Mum and Dad who needed to talk. Well, they said they did talk, but it wasn't exactly helping.

But here on the island everything has been fine.

Until now.

'There you are, you're petrified.'

Yes, here I am when Grandpa opens the door and squeezes his way into the little hallway. Petrified. Exactly right, Grandpa.

'What's wrong?' he says and takes hold of me.

He holds my arms tight.

'Look, you're on the front page.'

He lets me go and waves a newspaper in the air.

That's when I start to cry.

Then we sit at the table as usual, except today I am sitting next to Grandpa, with his heavy arm around my shoulders.

Grandpa has been making porridge and hugging me. Comforting me and saying he understands. He says it's tough. But he thinks everything is going to be all right. And then I relax a little, because Grandpa never promises anything, not like everyone else who always says they *know* things. He just says it's a tough situation, and you never really know what's going to happen, you can only hope. Have hope and faith. But he has spoken to Mum, and to Dad as well, and he tells me he thinks it's going to be OK.

'They're very right-minded people, your parents,' he says and smiles.

Though I wonder . . .

And then he takes out that newspaper again. The one he had hurried down to the harbour to get as soon as the morning deliveries came in. It hadn't occurred to him to write a note. Hadn't even occurred to him that I would wake up. Then Ylva was there standing by the fence.

'For a stop-and-chat,' he mumbles.

And he opens the paper out on the table. Points and shows me things and reads aloud, as if I can't read myself.

There's a big picture of the dead porpoise on the first page. And inside the big picture is a small picture of me. My red curls shine in the sun and I am squinting out from under the peak of my sailor's cap.

I think I look ridiculous, but Grandpa says:

'There she is – my captain.'

97

Then he grumbles about the fact box on whales. Says they've got lots of it wrong. Typical, he says. I should count myself lucky that they spelled my name right, at least.

Totally incompetent, apparently, those journalists.

Then he asks if I want to keep the paper. Put the picture up somewhere maybe?

But I reckon it would make good kindling for the stove.

Grandpa nods and the newspaper lands with a thud in the wood basket.

The next time I go down to the beach, it's empty. Birds sit quietly on their rocky ledges. No one is climbing the cliff. No sign of the porpoise. I wonder where it is now. I picture it in a hospital bed with slings and casts and needles in its fins.

I probably should have just left it there lying on the pebbles. Good food for the seagulls. Might have tempted that albatross down too. If it even exists. If it even eats porpoise.

It's not going to be any cooler today. The sea is dazzling, but the early morning air is cool and moist. A good time to get some work done, Grandpa says. And then have a lie-down under the lilac bush with our caps over our eyes and listen to the birds.

That's what he *says* he does – listen to the birds – but I know he's just napping. The birds don't have the energy to sing any more anyway.

More people pass by than usual this morning. Usually I'm the only one here, but now it seems that mini-whale has made this stretch of the beach famous. People want to come by and touch the pebbles. Inspect the spot where it happened.

When I tell Grandpa this he gets a little upset, in that way he does when he thinks something is silly.

'Ridiculous,' he says. 'Soon the council or that blasted history society will put up one of those obnoxious signs as well.'

He spits out the words.

I carry on with my boat. I've screwed in a new fitting for the mast. I'm pouring with sweat from the heat, even though I'm barely wearing anything. Just a vest. And my sailor's cap, obviously. Mum would go crazy if she saw my sunburnt shoulders. Now and then I have to go down and dip my head in the still water.

The birds are too hot to fly. They stay close to the rocks. But the Sand Witch comes over to say hello, eat a fried egg and then rest in the shade.

Still weird that it's eating a hen's egg, but it's better than plastic, I suppose.

Now and then I look up to see if she's coming. I notice my own impatience. It's just that I keep hearing footsteps.

Finally I go up to Grandpa. We sit on a blanket behind the lilac bush and enjoy some shade. Drink rhubarb lemonade and watch the swifts soaring above us.

'They live their whole lives in the air. Do everything there,' Grandpa says. 'Even sleep and mate. And if they land they can't take off again. Unless there's a height they can start from, like here.'

'The opposite of us then,' I say.

'Yes, you're right about that,' he says and smiles. 'The exact opposite of humans.'

Then he pulls his cap over his eyes.

'I'll just lie here and listen awhile,' he says.

Soon he's snoring. The birds are silent.

At the pub on Wednesday everyone wants to talk to me.

Earlier, I sat down at the kitchen table, as usual, watching as Grandpa paced around, as usual, with his sinewy, bendy body in a pair of baggy underpants pretending not to know what to wear.

Then we walked to the village. We didn't talk much, but Grandpa stopped from time to time to listen to things.

'There, did you hear that?'

It was a rosefinch in the Great Wood, he claimed, but I couldn't hear a thing.

Grandpa has taught me what to listen out for.

'*Pleased to meet you,*' says the rosefinch. In English.

This time it isn't Grandpa that everyone comes over to talk to at the pub. It's me. Everyone has a copy of the newspaper with me and the porpoise on the front page on their tables. Everyone's excited. But I mainly just reply with 'Um' and 'Well' and 'Yeah.' I wasn't even the one who saw it first. It was Ruth.

I spot her sitting over in the furthest corner. Same place as always. Arms crossed, black hat pulled low over her forehead. I try to go to her, but there are all these fat bellies in the way, bobbing up and down as their owners laugh and joke.

And as I squeeze myself through the fuss and waving newspapers and spilling, splashing beer, I see Ruth get up from her corner and run away. She moves past the rabble and I call after her from inside my prison of bobbing bellies:

'Ruth!' I shout.

And I know she must have heard me, but she just carries on out into the summer evening.

And then Ruth is just gone.

She doesn't come to the boat. Grandpa has started joining me. We're doing the last bits. There are quite a lot of last bits, but we've starting the oiling now.

Hot and sticky, but it smells good.

She isn't sitting on the cliff.

I turn my head up towards the lighthouse and stare. The sun tickles my nose and makes me sneeze.

Grandpa doesn't even say bless you. He just gets on with his tasks and mumbles sea shanties:

Way aye blow the man down . . .

But I'm worried.

There's not so much as a breath of wind.

In the evenings I might take the bike out for a ride around the island.

The bike is much too small for me now but I don't give a damn how I look. I cycle down to the village and pass the shop slowly. I look in through the windows, but it's always empty.

I cycle down to the harbour and walk out on the jetties.

Cycle up to the lighthouse, walk around the Great Wood, look down at the beach on the other side.

But she's gone.

And when I come back home to Grandpa, he is sitting by the lilac bush wondering where I've been. We have to go to Ylva's to call Mum. And Dad if I want. Which I do.

And, of course, Mum asks how it's going with that Ruth girl.
I say fine.

And Dad asks too, of course, because Mum told him that I
made a friend. That's the big news.

Best friend, I bet she says, because apparently they talk
about me.

I try not to sound angry but Dad can tell something is up.

So I say: 'We found a dead porpoise.'

But he's already heard that too. And about how I was in the
newspaper and all that.

Then I get tired of talking. Then Grandpa has to take over
and I sit there in Ylva's kitchen where it smells like something
is burning.

Grandpa is getting really into working on the boat.

But my mind is mainly on Ruth, who has disappeared. I walk around with my hands in my pockets, stroking the smooth surface of the shell inside with my thumb.

'Hold here,' says Grandpa and I take hold of the top of the mast so that he can detach the tattered old sail.

'Push here,' he says and I help him change the position of the boat so he can paint where he needs to.

'Pull here,' he says and I help him to align the rigging screws.

Then my hand goes back into my pocket.

And I can tell that Grandpa knows something is wrong.

'What's happened to your angel?' he asks in the evening as we're sitting with our tea, pipe and cards.

I just shrug.

'Fallen out?' he asks.

I shake my head, because we haven't.

'Maybe she went back to the city,' I say and try to look like I don't care.

'No, no,' he says. 'She is here for the summer. Like you. That's what I heard.'

Then I think: tomorrow. Tomorrow I will cycle to the shop and call on her.

What's the worst that can happen?

Grandpa is sitting at the table with a cup of coffee and a crossword. When he sees me his face lights up, he turns off what might be accordion music on the radio and goes to serve the porridge.

'Any dreams?' he asks, as usual, and I haven't the heart to tell him that I've been lying awake thinking. About people who disappear. Fathers, friends . . .

All the times I met Ruth down on the beach. All the days we sat there talking. All those quiet hours working on the boat. The way she smelled, breathed, felt. There was something going on inside me the whole time. Those fire sparks, leaping, burning, causing chaos – but in a good way.

All this time thinking about Ruth, waiting for her. And I never really minded her whining. And now she is just gone.

I had a best friend when I was little. His name was Kalle, but he moved to Arjeplog in Year 4 and I haven't had a proper friend since. I've always been the weird one, the outsider. Dad has always said it's the others who are weird and I'm the normal one, but I'm not sure. He probably stole that from some old song or something anyway.

He never shuts up about that, does Dad. He's always said how brave I am, even though I'm not at all.

'I think it's so cool that you have the confidence to be so colourful,' he would say and pat me on the sleeve of my brown and yellow chequered shirt.

All the while he would sit there dressed in blue and grey, sipping his black coffee.

'You do your own thing. Not everyone has the guts.'

The fact that I've never had proper friends, never brought anyone home after school, never had a sleepover, have always been quiet and boring, he has always twisted into a good thing.

But I know he worries.

'You'll find someone eventually,' he says, basically admitting that friends are the most important thing.

Mum has always tried to make me do activities where I could meet this *someone*. I've always said no. No to choirs and sports and film clubs; I really haven't wanted to.

And I have had friends. But no proper best friend, no gang, no one I've missed during summer holidays here on the island. No one who has ever asked if they can come along.

'Everyone needs a best friend,' I remember hearing Mum say to Dad one time. 'And a grandfather doesn't count.'

But over the last year she has stopped asking me about who I spoke to that day, or if there is someone at school I want to bring home or hang out with after school.

She's had other things on her mind.

And I've tried, I have, but it hasn't worked. I just haven't found a best friend. To be honest, I'm not sure I've really wanted to.

But then suddenly I find someone, or am found by someone, and maybe I'm still weird, but so is she, in a different way. And maybe it feels like we belong together anyway. And then she disappears. Ruth.

I try to act normal at the breakfast table with Grandpa but he can tell. I see him looking over at me now and then. But he mainly just talks about the weather. That it's still as hot as ever, stuff like that. He says it has to break soon and he is waiting for stormy clouds and thunderous downpours. He says he is expecting the worst storm since the twentieth century.

'You'll see,' he says.

I smile and hope.

'Then the sea birds might come to the island seeking shelter,' says Grandpa. 'The ones you never see.'

And he lists them again: petrel, northern gannet, albatross . . .

Grandpa suggests we go down to the beach and take a look at the boat. See what's left to do. But I tell him I have an important errand to do and I'm grateful that Grandpa isn't the type to ask questions. He just raises those enormous eyebrows slightly.

'Then I'll go out and do some work in the garden. It needs watering every day now.'

He just stands there with the hose, being my Grandpa. He waves to me above the drooping carrot tops as I cycle away in the direction of the Great Wood, Ylva's and the village. He just stands there with the hose, being my Grandpa.

I am wearing my sailor's cap, of course, and his old sailor's shirt. It's like a dress, with a sailor's collar and everything. But it has no pockets so my scallop shell is under my pillow. I could do with it now.

I brake on the gravel by the shop and prop the bike up against the wall.

Give a little wave to a few old men sitting on the bench with their coffee. After all these years, I still can't tell them apart. All the old men look the same at the pub on Wednesdays with their beer and peanuts. Or when they scurry around the dock when the boat comes in, loading up their carts and cargo mopeds with crates of drinks and bundles of newspapers. White hair and braces. Plaid shirts and tattooed arms. Only their bellies are different, some round and fat, others thin and muscly, all a bit stooped.

I start with the normal door, the one to the house where they live, Ruth and her granny. The house is kind of attached to the shop and is bigger than most others in the village, but just as white. I am breathing heavily as I stand on the pavement outside the door.

Heart fluttering, fingers trembling. But I'm here now. I ring the bell five times, but it's all quiet inside. Not a sound, no sign of movement.

'They're probably in the shop,' I hear one of the old men on the bench say and I turn around.

They gesture and point.

'The shop,' I hear again. 'Check in the shop.'

I raise my hand in thanks and walk slowly towards the shop. Can't back out now. Not with an audience. And word gets around on the island. That's what Grandpa says. 'Bloody gossip,' he says. And Mum says she can't stand that everyone knows everyone else's business. Still, she always smiles and acts sweet with the old men who call her a 'girl'. But then she leaves. Just takes off and leaves me to my fate.

The bell rings when I enter the shop and I see Ruth's granny straight away, standing behind the counter and writing something in a big ledger. She looks up and smiles when she sees me.

'Aha, you've come to pay us a visit. How lovely. What will it be today then? How are you doing up there?'

'Well,' I say. 'I just wanted to ask something.'

And then I bumble a bit. I don't understand why this is so hard. Just asking.

'What is it?' she asks and looks at me like I'm daft.

'Is Ruth home?' I manage to squeeze out.

'Yes,' she says. 'She's a little lazy in the mornings, that one. She's probably having breakfast about now. Go and ring the doorbell to the house and she'll answer.'

I feel a flutter in my stomach again. Ruth is here on the island. She is here.

Then I stand outside the front door and ring the bell again, but no one comes. I stand there for a long time pressing the button before I give up, cross the road and stand by the little tree there.

I look up at the house and see a sudden movement in one of the windows. The white curtain sort of flutters and I can see her standing behind it and looking at me. I wave but get no response.

'In the shop, we told you. She's in the shop.'

The old men are laughing at me and I can feel tears welling up.

I jog back over the road again, hop on the bike and go.

I hear the old men call after me. Something about porpoises and big discoveries.

By the Great Wood I have to stop and go in among the trees, to sit a while and let the tears flow. Then I have to sit a while and let them dry. Just breathing and blinking.

Then I hear that bird.

What was it that bird said in English again?

'Pleased to meet you.'

The rosefinch.

I'll have to tell Grandpa.

The Kiss

Here we are, sitting in the shade of the lilac bush, eating lunch. Sandwiches and a few freshly-dug carrots with a crunch of soil grit. Grandpa just stares up at the sky, waiting for that storm.

He's waiting for towers to form on the horizon, he says. For the clouds to grow tall and dark.

But they don't.

There is just pure blue. And the sun's harsh rays.

When I get up to go down to the beach and boat, I remind Grandpa that we have to call Mum and Dad today, but he doesn't take his eyes off the sky.

Walking down the steps, I look out for those clouds too. I am starting to look forward to an excuse to stay indoors with Grandpa and just play games and listen to the thunder. I would stand sheltered in the doorway and watch all the rare sea birds soaring and circling the lighthouse.

But everything is as usual. The beach is empty. The sun is blazing. I've given up on hoping Ruth will be there.

I get to work.

I have to attach rope ends to the new fittings. Grandpa has shown me how. We spend a whole evening practising the knots: bowline, half hitch, reef knot. He with his solid fingers: quick and nimble. Me with my bendy fingers: slow and fumbling.

'Well, if it isn't everyone's little hero!'

There she is, standing behind me and practically shouting in that thin voice of hers, full of rage. Her black shirt and hair are fluttering as she starts walking towards me. Threateningly.

'Huh?' I mumble, my heart pounding.

'The island's very own little celebrity,' she continues.

'What do you mean? Where have you been?'

'How could you?' she hisses.

'Could what? What have I done?'

I genuinely don't understand what she is talking about.

'You were in the newspaper: "the discoverer". You gave interviews like you were some sort of expert explorer. You didn't even mention me! Remind me who actually found that fucking seal?'

'Porpoise,' I correct her.

That was stupid.

'Well aren't you a fucking expert? Fucking Wikipedia kid.'

Saliva spits from her mouth. She hisses and shouts in turn. I can barely remember the last time I saw anyone this angry. She's acting like she might run up and smack me. I back up towards the boat.

'What? They came to me wanting to talk and ask questions. And I answered. I was looking for you but you disappeared.'

'It was *me* who found it. It was *me* who should have been in the paper. *Me* they should have interviewed on TV! *Me* who should have shown them where it was. *Me* they came and congratulated and interviewed. But you went ahead and took all the glory.'

I try to explain that I don't care about any of that; it just happened. She'd left the beach by the time I came back with Grandpa and then one thing led to another, when actually Grandpa and I would have much preferred to be left in peace. I tell her I looked for her but she was hiding. And it never crossed my mind that she would want to be in the newspaper or get

114

recognition from a bunch of identical old men with white hair and braces, because it wasn't a desire I could relate to.

'You must have known!'

She is on the verge of tears.

'You don't get famous just for finding a porpoise and appearing in the local newspaper,' I say.

But then she says she's looked it up and found the pictures in other papers too, bigger papers. I didn't even know there was internet out here.

'National papers,' she whispers.

Then I reply with a quiet 'Sorry' and edge towards her. She is standing with her hair hanging in her face and tears flowing down her cheeks.

'Sorry, sorry, sorry . . .'

And before she can say anything or push me away, I take her in my arms and hug her and stroke her hair. I feel the shoulder of my sailor's shirt moisten with her tears.

'It's all so unfair,' says Ruth.

And I tell her I was being thoughtless. I might go around with loud-print shirts and flaming hair but all I really want is to be left alone. And she might appear all in black, with her hair in her eyes, but what she wants more than anything is to be seen.

I apologise over and over again. Until I can barely remember why.

'We're super fucking different, you and me,' she says.

'I know,' I say and run my fingers through her hair.

It seems so daring . . . but feels natural.

We sit in the shade of the boat and she just sobs and sobs.

'So fucking different,' she says again. 'I wish I could be like you.'

'What? Like me? Why?'

Is she out of her mind?

'You make it look so easy,' she says. 'Everyone always says "just be yourself" and you're probably the only person I've ever met who actually is.'

I have to ponder this for a moment.

'But,' I say, 'if you were like me, then you wouldn't be yourself any more.'

She looks up. Tears stain her cheeks. She smiles.

'Well, who the hell am I then?'

And all of a sudden we're sitting there laughing and the tears begin to flow again.

Then we sit and compare. But the only conclusion we can come to is that no one is ever really satisfied. Everyone envies someone else. Everyone always thinks they are the ugliest, weirdest, most insecure.

Then I try to give her some suggestions, if she really wants to be famous.

'Mountain climber.'

'Ali and Astrid are already a thousand times better than me.'

'Explorer.'

'I hate the sea, remember?'

'Go on *Sweden's Got Talent*.'

'Oh yes, of course. And remind me what my talent is?'

'Suicide bomber.'

'Yeah, that's a no.'

'I've got it. You and I can be the first people in the world to sail around the world in a wooden sailing boat.'

She laughs.

Then I see what she's holding in her hand. Something white that she is stroking with her thumb. She looks up at me.

'Do you still have yours?' she asks.

I nod.

She turns to face me and comes up so close that I can feel her warm breath on my chin. I think she smells a little strange, kind of like the dentist's, and then her lips are on mine, her hand is behind my neck. I can feel the scallop shell there, cutting into my neck slightly. Her lips are surprisingly cold, but soft. My nose against her cheek . . .

'. . . Vinga! Vinga!'

I quickly pull away and get to my feet.

'Hi Grandpa!' I say weirdly loudly, so that Ruth will understand.

My heart is pounding so hard I'm sure it's visible through my shirt.

We stand side by side next to the boat. I feel crinkled, my hair abnormally ruffled. Do my lips look different? They're throbbing and hot. I pretend to fiddle with one of the knots on the stern as Grandpa comes over and stops on the other side of the boat.

'Sooo, the angel returns,' he says with a smile.

Then he turns to me.

'We should go up and make that phone call now,' he says.

I don't understand what the hurry is.

'I've still got a bit to do here,' I say and gesture vaguely at the boat.

I don't want to leave now. I want to stay here, with her. For ever.

But Grandpa gives me a look. One of those serious ones.

'Now, Vinga,' he says. 'Your mother's on the phone. We have to go to Ylva's.'

Dad

Grandpa rushes up the steps. Takes giant strides in his sandals. I scurry after with quick, small steps. I try shouting ahead to ask him what's going on, but he doesn't seem to hear. Just keeps taking three steps at a time. 'Come on,' I hear him say.

But then I stop and turn around to look at the boat and there she is, black and fluttering.

Ruth looks so small from up here, like an ant all the way down there by the boat, but I can tell she is looking at me. She raises her hand and smiles. And I do the same, raise my hand and smile. Then it feels like we're together.

And then this anxiety.

That it didn't mean anything.

That she wasn't taking it seriously.

That she was just trying it out.

That she was tricking me.

That she might just leave now. You know, *again*.

'Are you coming Vinga?!'

Grandpa is standing above me with his sailor's cap in hand. He wipes the sweat from his forehead on his sleeve. His grey hair is one big mess.

And I look down at her one more time. See how alone she is there. Down there, where I want to be.

And then I start running up to Grandpa and we rush over to Ylva's without speaking and if the birds are singing now, we don't hear them. If the albatross is swooping above the lighthouse now, we don't see it. Just the gravel path and hurried steps. Breathing and silence.

The heat in my lips. The memory in my body.

We get to Ylva's place, hurry through the garden and up to the house. She comes out to meet us on the front step and looks cheerful, though that doesn't seem appropriate.

Only then do I forget about Ruth. When my stomach turns. When my heart lurches and lands in the wrong place.

'Darling,' Mum begins.

'Stop that.'

'You have to come home.'

Then come the tears. I really don't want to.

'But, oh, I'm sorry sweetheart,' she says, but then remembers. 'No, sorry, *not* sweetheart. Well, I mean . . . Look, everything is fine, but you have to come home now.'

'What's happened?' I squeeze out, with fear in my heart.

'Well it's . . . the thing is . . . you've got a little brother.'

'Oh my god.'

'You've got a little brother. A cute little baby who wants to meet you.'

The tears come. I don't feel in the least bit happy. And I know that Mum is trying her best. A baby brother is supposed to be a happy thing, but it doesn't feel like mine.

It feels like all these tears have been out at sea and are just now rolling into shore on a wave. It feels like a whole world of forest fire and school and other catastrophes has crossed the sea and ruined everything. I knew this was coming, I knew that belly was swelling on the other side of the water.

But it has been so far away, somewhere else. Now it's right here.

And I don't want a brother. I don't want a new room and a new school and a new family.

I want Dad. And Mum. I want to be left in peace.

I can hear that Mum is making an effort but she doesn't sound happy. Not really.

She tells me again – she's been telling me a lot – how much

I longed for a little brother or sister when I was little.

'Well why didn't you give me one back then if you think it's such great news now? I don't want to come home. I can't.'

'Oh darling, I know.'

We go quiet. Her tears are quiet too.

I feel like I have a marble stuck in my throat, blocking the words from coming out. I just hand the phone to Grandpa and sit down on the floor.

Above me I hear Grandpa hum, see the seriousness in his eyes. See his knitted brow, though he attempts a smile when he looks at me. He doesn't look like Grandpa. Too old, too solemn. Weighed down, tired.

I sit on the floor and think about that new little person. I feel so sorry for him. He didn't know, he had no choice. He just appeared and now it doesn't feel like anyone really wants him. But then I think of Angelica. I can picture her glowing with happiness and saying loads of gross cutesy things in her hideous baby talk.

I'm just about to hope she had a really awful time pushing that baby out, when Grandpa looks down at me.

'Mum wants to say goodbye,' he says and hands me the phone.

I just breathe into it. It's warm on my ear and sounds crackly.

'Bye darling. I'll see you soon. Grandpa will bring you.'

'Love you,' I say.

It's all I can get out. It's the only thing that gets past the marble in my throat.

'And I love you. Always,' whispers Mum, and we hang up.

Then I look at Grandpa. Try to look questioning.

And he just nods.

'Yes, I'll take you. Let's go home and pack. We'll take the last boat this evening.'

On the way home from Ylva's, my heart is in a weird place. I'm barefoot, but I can feel that stone in my shoe, and in Grandpa's sandals. He just walks looking straight ahead, without a word. I think he's nervous.

Any typical grandpa would at least make an effort. Any typical grandpa would probably pat me on the back and say 'Congratulations' and 'Oh what fun to have a little brother'. But not mine.

We just walk along like two little storm clouds under the blazing sun.

I look up at the sky, at the soaring swifts, and listen out for their thin screeches. I can smell the dry heat and rotting smell of a motionless sea. Not a cloud.

'That storm . . .' I say.

'It's coming,' Grandpa says simply.

He is still looking straight ahead. Glassy eyes. It sounds so heavy when he says it.

'It's coming. Any day now.'

I wonder why Dad didn't call us himself and I imagine Mum sitting in the flat all alone.

She's the one who wants me to come.

She's the only one who needs me.

Grandpa has to go up into the loft to get his travel bag.

'I never thought I'd need this again,' he says and shows me a little chequered fabric bag with leather straps. It looks ancient and one side is covered with stickers: Valparaíso, Gran Canaria, Rio de Janeiro, Los Angeles, London, Rhodes, Cape Verde. Names bursting with adventure and freedom.

I laugh.

'Maybe just a *bit* old-fashioned.'

Grandpa's expression stays blank. No raised eyebrows, no secretive smile curling at the corner of his lips.

We pack in silence. I take my sailor bag, but figure I don't really need to take much. I have clothes in the city. And I'll be back here soon enough. We'll just go to the mainland to say hello and then everything will go back to the way it was. I have to believe this.

I turn around and see that Grandpa has put on his good suit. He notices me giving him a weird look.

'Mainland clothes,' he mumbles.

He is even wearing his tie. And just before the shipping forecast he even takes out a steel comb that I've never seen before and scrapes his hair flat against his scalp.

'Mainland hair,' I say, because I have to say something.

And on the weather report that afternoon they say nothing about storms or thunder. Only high pressure. Bright sun, gentle breezes.

'It's coming,' Grandpa says again and switches off the radio. And he takes out a yellow sou'wester for me and a grey one for him and that long oilskin coat that smells more like Grandpa than anything else and he slings it over his arm and we head out into the sunlight.

It is the first time in my whole life I see Grandpa lock his front door. The key is enormous. He hangs it up on a hook, right next to the door, but I don't point out how ridiculous that is. I just help him close the shutters.

Like the house is going to sleep.

Ylva comes to pick us up and we get on the rack of her quad bike. Grandpa sits all huddled up in his good suit and I think it's going to get dirty. Dust flies and the world shakes. Grandpa sits there clutching his travel bag on his lap and seems terribly uneasy. Knitted brow, distant gaze, quiet.

I wonder what's up with him. I wonder why it's so important for him to come with me. I've taken the boat alone before. I suspect it was Mum's idea and she asked him to bring me. Maybe she wants to see her father too.

Maybe deep down I'm glad to have Grandpa with me. But he seems so bloody nervous.

I know he doesn't want to come.

'Grandpa, when was the last time you were in the city?'

I shout the question but he still doesn't hear me. We'll just have to keep our mouths shut.

Ylva drives fast along the gravel roads and my stomach jitters and lurches, but feels heavy and hard at the same time.

When we get to the village, I'm on the lookout for Ruth. But it's just old men everywhere. Braces and cargo mopeds. Piles of newspapers and empty crates.

As we pass the house I look for what I think must be her window: nothing there. Just her granny peeking out curiously from the shop door. She probably keeps an eye on everyone who arrives on the boat. And everyone who leaves.

And I think again about what happened earlier today. Down there on the beach. I think about the kiss.

Because it was a kiss.

There's no mistaking it, even though it feels very distant now.

I don't understand how it happened and it feels like it was days ago already. Like the memory should have faded. But I still feel it on my lips. Cool and hot. Soft. The taste, like at the dentist's.

It felt perfectly natural at the time. Now it seems like the most bizarre thing that has ever happened.

The quad bike brakes suddenly. It jolts Grandpa and me. He is still clutching tight onto his bag.

'We're here,' says Ylva. 'We made it.'

She helps Grandpa down from the rack and I take his travel bag. I ask why he has packed so much. He'll probably be back in the morning.

Then he looks up at the sky, then towards the horizon, then at me.

'You never know,' he says. 'You never know how long you'll be away once you've set off.'

Then he takes me to one side. We walk a few steps until we can see the lighthouse behind the trees. Then he nudges me and points.

'Here it comes,' he says. 'What did I tell you? Here it comes.'

And I look up towards the lighthouse but don't see anything. Just the same clear blue sky. Just the same swifts surging through the air. Just the same baking hot sun.

'What?'

'Just look,' he says.

So I look. And I see it.

An enormous white bird with wide, dark wings is flying high up by the lighthouse. A few soaring circles, the occasional wingbeat, then it swoops down to land on the railing at the top.

'The albatross,' whispers Grandpa. 'Here comes the thunderstorm.'

Grandpa steps aboard the boat with his old chequered travel bag in one hand and me in the other. The captain comes down from the jetty, walks over to Grandpa and shakes his hand. He asks what's going on. Is Grandpa sick? Surely he isn't leaving the island?

'Ten years,' mumbles Grandpa and it takes me a while to realise that this is in response to the question I tried to ask on the quad bike earlier.

'I haven't left in ten years,' he says.

'Then it's definitely high time,' the captain laughs.

He's big and fat, the captain, with gold embroidery on his jacket. He is supposed to look elegant and important, but his clothes are dirty and crumpled, and his tie is twisted, and fuzzy black hair spills out of his collar. His beard is messy and his cap is crooked.

Grandpa looks glumly at the fat man in gold. He doesn't offer any more explanation. He points to the horizon and says the storm is coming.

'You should probably hurry and set sail.'

But the captain just laughs again.

'A storm? You must be sick after all.'

He sort of hums and points at the calm, glistening water.

Then Grandpa walks past him. I can still hear the captain laughing behind me.

Grandpa wants to sit inside but I stand out on the deck. I watch the island get smaller and smaller and the water swirl and foam around the boat. I look up at the lighthouse but can't see the albatross. Was that really it? Did I see it? Was it just my imagination?

Over on the jetty, where we just came from, lots of old men in braces are packing up quad bikes, cargo mopeds and tractors. Summer visitors need driving to their rented cottages. Food supplies for the shop. Tools for the fishermen and farmers.

But then I see something black and fluttering come running up the jetty. I see people turning to look at her as she comes. I've never seen her move so quickly. She's running and it looks like she doesn't plan on stopping. Like she might run all the way to the end of the jetty, ripping off her clothes as she runs, dive in and swim after the boat.

But she doesn't.

She sort of skids to a halt, like a cartoon character, and stops dead at the end of the jetty where she stands panting and staring after us. I raise my arm to wave.

But she just stands there staring as the boat swings round the headland and she shrinks smaller and smaller until eventually she is hidden behind the rocky land and all I see is the pebble beach. And there's the sailing boat. She has pulled the tarpaulin over it, just like me and Grandpa do. She has put rocks on so it won't blow away, it looks like.

The boat pulls away from the island. Everything shrinks. I see the cliff and the lighthouse and the beach, just about. That's all. I can't see the steps or the roofs of the houses. No birds. Soon the whole island is just a little lump of rock on the horizon.

That's when I feel the first breath of wind. It's cold. I shiver.

I look out across the water and see that ripples have started to form, small waves even. And when I look at the horizon I see them.

The clouds.

Big blue-grey clouds, some almost purple, billowing tall like smoke, slowly swelling from the horizon. They look shiny. Almost polished. Like enormous bruises on the sky.

The clouds drift as if in slow motion, but it's still obvious that they're growing fast. They're alive.

And coming closer.

We're sailing straight towards them.

I go inside to join Grandpa and he looks kind of happy all of a sudden. Raised eyebrows, shining eyes staring at the horizon. A contented smile on his lips.

'What did I tell you!?'

He doesn't look at me as he says it. He can't take his eyes off the horizon. He points at some birds on their way to the island to seek shelter from what's coming. He names them: velvet scoter, guillemot, auk. Asks me if I've ever seen a storm petrel. Or a northern gannet.

I just shake my head.

Grandpa had a northern gannet once, he says, that always came back to the same spot. Every year it would sit at the furthest point on the jetty where he would often dock his boat. That was on Bornholm, he says, and they became friends, he and the bird. He says it would look at him in a special way. Like it recognised him and almost smiled when he appeared on the jetty. Cocked its head to one side and opened its pointy beak slightly, as though in greeting.

'They look like they're having too much fun to be those northern gannets,' he says and I can tell from his expression that his mind is far away.

And then I think about the Sand Witch, of course. And I hope that Ruth will go back sometimes, to the boat. Sit there and talk to the Sand Witch anyway. And that maybe she will miss me just a little bit. That's all.

'Then one day it was gone,' says Grandpa.

He is still talking about that bird.

I'm just about to ask him about it when there is a sudden

bang and the boat shakes. I have to grab onto Grandpa to steady myself.

Grandpa's chequered travel bag, which he only just dared let go of, crashes to the floor, colliding with a panting little black dog. The dog barks, a small child falls from their seat. The deck door opens and everyone who is still outside pours in.

Now suddenly rain is whipping against the windows, or the portholes, as Grandpa calls them, and the waves keep coming. And they're just getting bigger and bigger. I hurry over towards the dog and snatch the travel bag. I almost fall over with every step I take. The boat is lurching quickly, back and forth, back and forth.

Slower and slower. Deeper and deeper. What started as small, irregular jolts have become an intense, steady rhythm. I am very aware of my heart in my chest. Racing. Not at all in rhythm with the long, deep movements of the boat. And I have to keep swallowing because my mouth is strangely dry.

When I come back to Grandpa he is smiling. Glowing. He looks happy! I sit down next to him and he looks at me with shining eyes, nodding nodding nodding.

I look over at the island. It looks like a glowing mountain on the horizon. The sun is still shining over there. But dark grey is spreading across the water and soon the island is enveloped in darkness as well.

Everything outside the window turns grey. Almost black. You can't even see the water. Or rather, you can't see anything but water. Rain rain rain. It splashes up, high above the windows. The waves wash over the deck.

Then a voice comes over the tannoy. It's the captain. He

says that no one could have predicted this. Then he pauses and adds: 'Well . . . except one person.' Then he says that no one is to open the doors. There's no need to be concerned. He's seen worse. But under no circumstances should anyone go outside or open any doors. If everyone stays inside and sits down and maybe holds onto something, he will make sure we get safely to land.

But still, he sounds nervous. His voice.

Then Grandpa laughs loudly.

'Not laughing now, is he? Him up at the helm,' he says loudly.

I notice the way people look at us. Anxious. And I'm going to be a sailor. I'm not supposed to get frightened.

I'm supposed to be like Grandpa. Someone who thinks this is the life. How do I become like him? I'm trying my best not to be scared, but I can hardly breathe.

I glance subtly, so that Grandpa can't see, up at the wall above us where a sign says what to do in case of emergency. I try to figure out where the lifeboats are, what's the deal with life jackets. Feel carefully under the wooden bench. There's something there. Something hard and cloth-like.

But how do these life jackets work? How long can you survive in this water? And what if I drown? And Grandpa. In his nice suit. Shit.

What would happen to Mum? If we died.

The boat continues to sway. Water lashes and crashes, thunders and thumps, as it pours over the railing and washes the deck shiny and clean.

On the bench opposite us someone rushes to the toilet, bent double. Grabbing whatever handhold they can find along the way. Someone else suddenly jumps up and vomits into a bin and the smell fills the boat. Sighs and groans. And that child, who fell before, is on its dad's lap screaming and screaming. Other than that no one makes a sound. No one speaks. Only the dad whispering soothing words to his child, even though he looks terrified himself.

Then a bang. And another message from the bridge.

'This is the captain again. We've run into a little problem with one of our rudders, but nothing to worry about. Rest assured that the crew on this vessel are highly experienced and have dealt with far worse situations. However, as a safety precaution, we have to travel at a limited speed. Please remain seated and hold on if you need to, and we will make sure we bring you safely to shore.'

I try to swallow but I can't. Grandpa looks at me.

'Take it easy, captain. It's probably nothing. Like he said, he's seen worse. And you'll see worse too. This is hardly the *Bluebird*.'

He laughs.

'But what's going on? We could sink any minute,' I whisper.

But Grandpa is still grinning like a kid on Christmas Eve.

'This is just the beginning,' he says. 'The storm. It's coming.'

Then we hear the first clap of thunder.

138

'I think they might need a little help up on the bridge. What do you say, captain? Shall we bring this little boat in to land?'

The wreck of the *Bluebird*. *Doomed to ruin.*

Crew only.

Grandpa steps straight over the chain and walks up the stairs. Then he turns to me. I stay where I am, clutching the handrail. I'm starting to feel a bit nauseous but try not to think about it. I keep an eye out for places to throw up. The toilet is locked and several people are waiting. Pale, blank faces all in a row. Other people's vomit is already dripping from the bin. It smells like petrol and bile.

Grandpa calls from up the steep staircase:

'Come on. Now! Crawl underneath. Those silly signs don't count for sailors. Hold on.'

He opens the door with another sign on it.

No entry for unauthorised persons.

'Unauthorised,' he scoffs. I hurry to catch up.

There is a low, continuous humming noise up on the bridge. A thick, soft carpet on the floor. Large framed nautical charts on the walls and windows in all directions. Outside, just grey. No visibility beyond a metre.

Grandpa comes storming in and the captain whips around without letting go of the wheel.

'It's you,' he says. 'Fine, come in. But you shouldn't be here.'

Grandpa just smiles and looks at him.

'Shouldn't I?'

'Fine. Come in. Shut the door.'

The captain gives me a quick, disapproving look.

He's pale in the face. But he has to keep looking ahead. Hands on the wheel.

'Are you the only one here?' asks Grandpa.

The captain makes a small head movement. Nods towards the door. Lying on the couch over there is a young man in a blue suit just like the captain's but with less gold. He is throwing up into a bin.

The captain sighs.

'Shit, I don't know what to do. It came on so suddenly. No one was prepared. Nothing on the radio. No reports from land. What is this?'

'Just a bit of weather,' says Grandpa.

'A bit? I've never seen the like. It's a damn hurricane!'

'Barely a storm. Just a gale. But getting worse,' Grandpa replies calmly.

Just then comes another bang, but not from the boat this time. Immediately after the bang the whole world lights up with a sudden flash of gold.

The captain undoes his top shirt button. Sweat is trickling down his podgy cheeks. Or they might be tears.

And just like that, Grandpa is steering the boat. He is glowing as he waves me over. The captain has given up and is sitting on the edge of the sofa where his helmsman is being sick.

Now it's me and Grandpa in our sailor's caps at the helm. Grandpa shows me various levers and buttons and the screen flashing in front of the steering wheel. But he says we don't really need it. We know these waters. And then he winks in that way of his.

'Right, captain!'

It feels a bit better up here. Now that I can see out. My heart is still hammering in my chest, but it feels a little safer now that Grandpa is in charge.

Suddenly Grandpa speeds up and turns towards the enormous waves.

'What are you doing? Hold course!' we hear from the sofa.

'Oh hush,' says Grandpa. 'We know where we're going. But we don't want to take any risks. We have to cross the waves a little.'

The captain looks horrified but he must trust Grandpa anyway because he makes no attempt to get up. He just sits there, hunched over. His enormous stomach jiggles up and down.

And now I can actually feel things growing calmer. The side-to-side rocking of the boat slows down when Grandpa changes course. Instead we move slowly up and then quickly down. Our speed increases. There is another bang, followed by a flash of light.

'It's right above us now,' Grandpa says calmly.

The captain is trying to catch his breath on the sofa.

I feel weird and kind of sick. But I really don't want to throw up. Grandpa would be so disappointed. I sit down by his feet, lean against the wall under the windows and imagine the horizon, like Dad taught me. It smells musty here. Cold and clammy.

I shut my eyes and there he is: Dad . . .

At first I didn't understand. Everything was more or less the same as usual. It was winter and I was dreaming of the furthest islands in the sea. Thinking about the ice and seals and birds sitting there all alone waiting for the light to return.

I was walking through the forest on my way home from school. It was dark and cold and wet, and I wondered what it was like under the ice. Where life was just carrying on. And further out, where the ice ended and the water became black and dangerous. And even further, where the whales were still swimming free and travelling south to other parts of the infinite ocean, where it might be summer and warm and filled with jumping dolphins and floating manatees.

I thought about oceanic trenches and giant squid. Coral reefs, moray eels, harbours on the other side of the world. There was so much more out there, somewhere else entirely, and I was walking through the forest, having taken a detour home to avoid everyone. I would never take the tram with the others. In the forest I could be alone. I was cold. Not even the residents of the nursing home were walking out there now. They'd probably slip and break something.

Sometimes Dad would come and meet me in the park. He would look so happy to see me and call out my name so loud I got embarrassed, even though there was no one around to see or hear. Maybe, like, one old man walking his dog.

'I needed a walk,' Dad would say. 'Can't get any decent work done today anyway.'

But he didn't ask about school any more. He knew.

We just walked along and stopped at a cafe. He drank a

coffee and I had orange soda. We sat at our usual table and talked about everything under the sun. Just not school.

Back home Dad usually had to get back to work.

'There are a few things I need to get out of the way,' he said and shut himself in his office.

I lay down on the bed and looked at my nautical map. Got out my phone and watched some TV show or other, which was never as good as people said it was.

Sometimes I'd take a book from the pile by my bed and read a few lines.

May I borrow your tail for a few days
to shade myself from the dark?
Dear Squirrel!

Was this the kind of thing Dad read? Thought I should read?

At least the man on the cover reminded me of Grandpa a little.

When Mum came home dinner was ready and we ate and then Dad cleared up and Mum just talked about work and maybe we would watch something on TV and the days just went by.

As usual.

Or so I thought.

But something was up. Dad stopped meeting me in the park as often. I started coming home to a dark, empty flat more often. With only the Christmas lights on in the window and a luminous nativity scene in the kitchen. Dad put it up every year even though Mum thought it was the ugliest Christmas decoration she'd ever seen.

'Hideous,' she always said. 'Did you make it at school or something?'

Then Dad would get really upset.

'You know it belonged to my grandmother,' he said. 'You know it has to be there. It wouldn't be Christmas without it.'

And I agreed. It had always been there.

'I know,' said Mum. 'It's just so ugly.'

She said she had to put up with a lot of things for our sake. But she smiled as she said it.

'You're going to have to put up with us for ever,' Dad replied.

But that wasn't true and he must have known that.

Mum and I started making dinner ourselves and eating without him more often.

Dad was so busy suddenly. He had meetings and trips and all sorts of Christmas dinners, he said.

Sometimes I heard him come home late when I was lying in bed trying to sleep. Then I heard Mum ask questions.

'Where have you been this time? Are these dinners really that important? Why are you out all the time?'

'I'm not, it's just . . .'

And so it began.

Often I didn't even hear him come home and sometimes

he was already gone when I woke up. Then Mum got cross when I asked about it.

'He's very busy at the moment, apparently,' she said. 'But I don't know . . .'

And then it was a hurry to get out the door.

I would take the forest path, as usual, to avoid the others.

Often arrived late to school. Said sorry, excuse me, and went and sat down.

And just put up with it.

And then there were the fights.

It started with talking and muttering behind closed doors, which continued and intensified, just like the wind, rain and thunder now. The breaking of the storm.

The way Dad shouted at Mum to calm down.

The way Mum shouted back and cried.

Doors banging, someone left.

It was almost always Dad who left.

The way he stopped sleeping at home.

The way he met me in the park again and hugged me and seemed happy to see me. Walked me home, but rarely stuck around to cross paths with Mum.

And of course I asked what was going on, but apparently it was too difficult to explain. Everything was going to be fine, we just needed to give it some time. We just needed to give Mum some time. Or give Dad some time. And they tried. Those dinners we had together when they tried to act normal and talk about all the stuff that people talk about, but which felt pointless.

And those long phone calls I overheard Mum having. And her crying.

The day I came home and it was all dark. That was the last day of school. The beginning of the Christmas holiday.

The kitchen was pitch-black, the nativity scene was gone. I found it later. Broken in two out by the recycling bins.

Mum bought a new one in metal.

This one was beautiful, she thought.

That Christmas was the worst.

'Captain, captain. Land ahoy!'

I am wrenched out of my thoughts by Grandpa's voice. It might have been minutes or hours, I don't know.

The captain and helmsman are lying on the sofa in a pile of blue and gold.

I get up and stand next to Grandpa at the helm. Everything is still grey outside. The waves are enormous, but flatter now, and longer.

Everything still feels uncertain and dangerous, but it's almost making me feel calm.

I look at Grandpa and my breathing slows. Here we are now, me and him, in the eye of the storm. He smiles.

In the distance, through the misty grey, I see something dark sticking out from the water.

'That's the pier.' Grandpa points. 'Now we just need to come into harbour and dock without damaging anything.'

'Well, that's my job,' says the captain, getting up from the sofa with effort.

He puts on his cap. His beard is messy and his face is white. He holds his hands out to Grandpa but doesn't thank him for the help.

'It was very generous of me to let you steer for a bit. Had fun, did you?' he said instead.

I look at Grandpa, but he just laughs and lets the captain take over.

When we come down from the bridge we're struck with the sharp smell of vomit. Bags lie strewn about the floor and passengers are draped over benches and trolleys and suitcases.

The father with the young kid is sitting curled up in a corner clutching his child. He has put a life jacket on. Pictures have fallen off the walls and the toilet door is banging open and shut. It's utter chaos but no one says a word. I turn to look at Grandpa. Has someone died down here or something?

Grandpa just smiles.

'It's all right everybody. Up you get, we'll soon come into harbour. The captain is just about to dock the boat and then you'll have to return to land for the time being. Hasn't he done a great job, your captain?'

Then people begin to stir. They sit up and straighten their clothes, smooth down their hair. Wipe the corners of their mouths, rub a little life into their faces. Then huge, frightened eyes all turn to Grandpa and someone starts clapping quietly. And suddenly Grandpa and I are standing there on the stairs as more and more of the passengers stand up, turn to us and applaud. Someone shouts bravo. Someone whistles.

We're like rock stars now.

And then we hear the engine screech, the boat lurches to the side one last time, and then there is a proper bang when the boat meets the big decking on the quay. And another one. And another. Then suddenly all is still.

Nothing comes over the speakers, but the door behind us opens and the helmsman walks slowly down the stairs. Me and Grandpa make space for him to pass. He has large flecks of vomit on his crumpled white shirt. His face is white as chalk as he ploughs his way through the crowd and opens the door. He makes some sort of arm movement. As if to tell us we can get off now. Then he hurries out, before everyone else. The storm pulls him inland as he jogs away from the boat, the pier, the sea.

I watch him go, but he disappears somewhere around the big car park.

And that's when I see her.

She is standing there by a little red Toyota and waving.

Mum.

'What are you doing here? Me and Grandpa were going to take the train. It was all decided.'

We have struggled our way to the car park and the little red car and Mum. The wind and rain whipping and lashing our faces. Only when we have hugged hello and got in the car does Grandpa take out the sou'westers.

'Bit late now,' he mumbles and stuffs them back in the pocket of his oilskin coat.

'Yes,' Mum says. 'It was decided. But then this storm came.'

Mum says she heard warnings on the radio. That major train delays should be expected.

'I was very worried,' she says.

Then me and Grandpa look at each other.

'About us!' he says and laughs. 'Worried about us? You must be joking. We were having great fun out there. A bit of proper weather was just what this summer needed.'

Grandpa turns to me. I'm sitting alone in the back seat, thinking that I've never seen Grandpa so happy and excited. And I'd never seen him as grim and glum as when we were about to leave the island.

Then comes a storm and it's like he doesn't have a care in the world.

'And there was another thing,' Mum says from the front seat.

I see in the rear-view mirror that tears are running down her face. I can see that she is crying.

'I missed you both so much,' she says and when Grandpa touches her cheek she starts sobbing.

And then I start too.

My heart again. Fluttering and fighting.

Fuuuck, I want to scream. I want to stamp, kick and punch, but I don't know what to do with myself so I just sit in the back seat crying quietly. It's all happening inside me.

And we're so far away from the island now.

And Ruth . . .

In the front Mum and Grandpa are talking softly. I'm not listening. Outside, heavy rain is falling, the windscreen wipers are thrashing back and forth but it barely helps. The pine trees along the side of the road look like they might fall on us at any moment.

Outside, dusk is falling and it feels like for ever since that moment on the beach. The kiss.

It was this afternoon. Only a few hours ago. The sun, the boat, the Sand Witch, the sea. And Ruth and her tears. Our laughter. And that kiss. The heat.

Yes, for ever.

And I feel something like panic.

'I want to go back,' I whisper through tears, thinking of the sea, the summer, the island.

Grandpa hears me:

'Me too, Vinga. Me too.'

And Mum is sitting in the front seat. Mum, who must be so damn lonely all the time.

Everything was supposed to be like it was before. But I could tell from the way Mum spoke that it wasn't. She was avoiding eye contact and acting weird.

She knew everything had gone to shit.

The words that suddenly started appearing here and there and the raised voices and the tears and Dad's wardrobe slowly being emptied. He never brushed his teeth at home any more.

Everything became so serious and bleak and Mum swore and screamed in the morning and then we would stand in the hallway before we said goodbye for the day and hug. She said she was sorry and felt ashamed of herself.

When Dad was home they smiled with their lips but not their eyes and said that everything was going to be OK.

'This will pass. We'll figure it out.'

'It's not your fault,' Mum would always say in the evenings when she sat on my bed and said goodnight and thought I seemed sad.

As if I ever thought it was my fault.

And then, bit by bit, he disappeared, my dad. A shirt here, a book there. Like he thought we would feel it less if he just took a little at a time, like it wouldn't be as obvious that he was abandoning me. But it was obvious. I thought about it all the time. How someone who had always been there could just disappear. I thought about it constantly. What could he have somewhere else that was so much better or more important? I missed him so much it hurt.

I might be sitting there in class and fantasising about the great beyond when tears would just start coming and suddenly it felt like everyone was looking at me. All those classmates who were usually too wrapped up in their own lives.

At first I skipped the odd lesson, then whole days. I would mainly just hang around in town. Sit in various places drinking tea, listening to music: 'The Eel' on repeat. I went to the cinema. Wished I was somewhere else.

Sometimes Grandpa called in the evenings and we would just sit there, on either side of an endless sea, in silence. Which helped, actually.

I wonder what Ylva thought then, in her kitchen with its smell of burning.

One day Dad was waiting outside school when I finished. My heart leapt when I saw him across the road and I scurried over like a squirrel and almost got run over. But he just laughed.

'Oh, I'm so happy to see you,' he called and hugged me tight.

'Me too,' I said.

And I really was just happy to see him, despite all the anger and confusion I'd been feeling. I wanted to ask him how he could do this to us, but of course I didn't. His big smile. I felt all warm inside.

'I've missed you so much!' he said after we'd hugged and stood there looking at each other and smiling.

Dad had a brand new scarf, which he was very proud of. It was big and red. He showed it off and let me wear it, even though it hung almost all the way to the ground on me. But it smelled really good.

'Just knitted,' he said.

Then he asked if I wanted to go to Cafe Zenith for a drink.

I did want to and we walked arm in arm, passing my so-called classmates but I couldn't care less if they were looking at me and I didn't listen to whatever they were saying. Just saw their mouths moving.

Then we sat there, Dad with his coffee, me with my orange soda, and he told me what he was up to. Work. I wanted to ask about something else but didn't want to break the mood. But then he changed the subject.

'So, Vinga,' he said. 'How are you doing?'

'Good.'

'Really? So why are you skipping so much school? You know that . . .'

I looked down at my leopard-print trousers and my hair fell in my eyes and I spoke in a whisper.

'But you're not coming home . . .'

'Oh, Vinga.'

He got up, came round to my side of the table and sat there crouched down. I used his red scarf to wipe my eyes.

'Why won't you come home?'

'It's complicated,' he said.

And he said it again, all that stuff about how none of this was my fault and all he really wanted was to be with me. That he was sorry things had turned out this way and that I was the most important thing, until I just wanted to scream . . .

'Hiya,' said a voice from behind us and I saw Dad kind of stiffen.

She was just standing there with an enormous smile. Jet-black hair and big hoop earrings.

'Hiya,' she said again. 'Am I disturbing?'

'Maybe a little,' said Dad. He sounded uncertain and looked at me.

But then he smiled.

'Vinga, this is Angelica,' he said.

She leaned down and patted me on the hand.

'So lovely to meet you, Vinga,' she said, like she was talking to a baby.

I snatched my hand back. I felt violated.

Angelica had a distinct smell. She smelled exactly like the scarf.

I was already sick of that smell.

That evening was the first time I had one of those episodes where I couldn't move and my heart was in completely the wrong place.

When I came to, Mum was standing in the door with tears in her eyes, shouting at me.

When Dad and I went to the cinema, Angelica wasn't allowed to join us. Dad wanted me to come over to his house sometime. But he lived with her. So I didn't want to.

Mum said I absolutely didn't have to.

It was spring but Dad was still wearing that scarf, and no doubt sweating.

When he came home, to our home, he hung it up on the hook in the hall and its smell stank up the whole flat. Mum and I whispered by the balcony door and laughed about the fact that we had both thought the same thing, but Dad didn't get the joke.

Sometimes it was OK having Dad there. We could eat together, even though it was Mum who cooked. Like Dad didn't dare. Suddenly he was a guest.

Usually after dinner we'd sit in my room, me and Dad, while Mum cleared up. We might play something, but we didn't talk much.

When he left he always took something with him. A book, or a pair of shoes he had dug out of the wardrobe, or his favourite cup, the one with Kermit the Frog on it. Slowly he removed any trace of himself from the flat.

Afterwards, Mum seemed empty but happy. We hugged. The kitchen was sparkling clean. She had been in there pretty much all evening.

The radio was on and broadcasting the shipping forecast.

I longed for summer.

Then I could be with Grandpa out on the island for several weeks, they'd promised.

I must have fallen asleep in the back of the car eventually, because I wake up with a start when Mum turns the engine off. It's getting light again, but the storm is raging on, howling.

On the other side of the road, by the park, big branches have been blown off the trees, and paper, plastic and other bits of rubbish are hovering and swirling like ghosts. It feels like we've been driving for half the night.

We go up to the flat and have some tea and toast before bed. Mum and Grandpa argue over where he will sleep. He insists the sofa is fine but Mum says he should take the bed. Obviously Grandpa wins and when I come to say goodnight he is already lying there snoring in his nice suit.

I'm not sure how long I've been away from home, but when I come into my bedroom it feels like for ever. I recognise everything, obviously. It looks just like it did before.

The nautical chart on the wall, the globe in the window. The ugly striped rug on the floor and all the tatty old cuddly toys sitting in a neat row on my bed, waiting for the love they might never get again. Everything is like it was before, except not.

I shut the door, lie down on my red bedspread and look up at the ceiling.

There comes a knock on the door. And I remember that knock. From last spring. When Mum wanted to come in for serious talks. About Dad and Angelica, about me and my weird episode. About doctors, psychologists and poets. And conversations that turned into nothing but yes, no, maybe . . .

Then Mum comes in. She is walking lightly in that way she does when it's something important. She has made tea and puts my cup down on the bedside table. It's the one with Moomintroll on it.

'Your favourite cup, right? I've been borrowing it while you were away,' she says and sits down next to me on the bed. She strokes my forehead and cheek and says, 'Ohhh.'

And then she tells me she has spoken to Dad. He wants me to come.

'What about you?' I say.

'We'll see.'

'Don't you want to?'

'Yes and no, I think.'

'Me too.'

'He *is* your brother.'

'Not a full brother.'

And she says she understands that I want to go back to the island, to my simple life there. To summer.

'But Dad really wants you to come. And I need you here with me.'

'OK,' I say. 'Go away now.'

And then I lie there in bed and look at the nautical chart. If you continue west you can reach the Hebrides. Grandpa showed me. That's where you have to go, he says. It's the final outpost, after that it's just open sea.

People are all crowded together on land, in the cities, living squashed together, tightly squeezed, like pages in a thick book. But out there, out at sea, you're free. Above you is only air and sky, stars and the infinite beyond them. Below you is the

161

deep, the unexplored depths where no human can survive. Only whales, krill and crabs.

The deep waters are shown on the chart as numbers, but what those 652 metres are hiding, nobody knows.

In the morning I sit with Grandpa on the sofa at home in the flat. Now I understand why we were in such a hurry to get off the island; our boat was the last to depart before the storm. Everyone on the island is stranded for the time being and Grandpa knew it. Ruth can't leave. She hates life on that island and now she really is a prisoner. And I'm here.

Now I understand why Grandpa packed so much into that old-fashioned travel bag of his. He can't go home. On TV they're talking about the storm, accidents, cancelled trains and flights. Winds of up to seventy miles per hour. Everyone has to stay inside, they say. Roofs and tiles can blow off. No one seems to know when it's going to calm down.

And no one seems to know what's happening in the forests either. Fires are still burning in some places.

'Potentially fatal,' says a rescue leader.

'Disaster,' says the prime minister.

Meteorologists show maps and point and say maybe this, maybe that, but no one dares say anything for certain.

Only Grandpa.

'Another day or so,' he says. 'Another day or so. Then the boats can start up again. Then the summer will return.'

We talk about the island and wonder how Ylva is doing, and the sheep and the albatross and the sailing boat. We travel there in our minds and then Grandpa's forehead wrinkles in that way it does and I know he would much rather be there. He loves storms at sea. I can picture him now, dancing around beneath the lighthouse, laughing at the rain and thunder and storm.

But instead he is sitting here. Shut up in a tiny flat by a park in the city. On a sofa with the TV on and a broken-hearted daughter and a miserable granddaughter. Talk about disaster.

Then I say it:

'I want to go back with you.'

'What?'

'You know, when the weather is better. In a day or so. When the boats have started again. I'm going back with you to the island.'

He looks at me and smiles. Raises his eyebrows.

Then he just laughs.

'All right, captain. All right.'

At breakfast I check the weather in the newspaper. We've missed the shipping forecast on the radio.

Mum sweeps past behind me, on her way to serve Grandpa more coffee. Grandpa just looks at me and nods.

'Check when the storm is supposed to die down,' he says. 'If they think they're so smart, those experts.'

Mum sits down opposite me.

'I still can't believe you were in the newspaper this summer, darling. So cool,' she says. 'You must have saved a copy. Can I see?'

Then we look at each other, Grandpa and me.

'It made good kindling,' says Grandpa. Mum gets something caught in her throat and has to stand up and cough.

Then Mum tries to lighten the mood around the breakfast table. Asking all sorts about the island. About the porpoise and Ylva and the old men with their trousers and braces. How are Yngve and Gunnar and the Österman brothers? What do we eat out there? Do they still have that pub on Thursdays?

'Wednesdays,' I mumble and Mum immediately takes interest and asks more.

Grandpa looks uncomfortable. He really can't stand this sort of small talk. I just mumble in response to all of Mum's questions.

Mmm, sure, yes, no, not yet, yeah . . .

Mum tires of us and starts reading the paper instead.

Then after a little while she puts the paper down again, rests her elbows on the table and sort of launches towards me with a wide-eyed whisper:

'Hey. What about Ruth? Your new friend. I'm sure you've got plenty to tell me about her.'

I freeze. I feel butterflies deep in my belly, just like on the back of Ylva's quad bike. I get all hot inside and then the heat rises and I feel my neck going red and it keeps rising higher and higher . . .

Stop it, I think, stop it, but it just keeps going and my cheeks get hot and Mum's eyes are bright and her smile is wide and now I can feel Grandpa looking up from his porridge and his paper and watching me as well like he's waiting for me to answer.

My mouth goes dry and I can feel my eyes darting around, despite myself. I stare at that sticker that has been on the kitchen cupboard door since for ever. A whale. Mum has tried scraping it off but that only made it worse. Still there. If a little grubby.

'She's truly an angel, that girl.'

Grandpa has answered for me. He got there first. He rescued me. He laughs, then I start laughing too.

Then we're sitting there laughing again, me and Grandpa, and Mum almost looks a little sad.

She's on the outside, again.

And before I know it, here we are. Outside this door I'm supposed to open.

I've tried talking my way through the hospital corridors. I've told Mum all about those huge sperm whales. About their brains – the biggest in the world – and their lonely journeys through the ocean.

As if she cares.

I suppose I've been talking to avoid thinking about everything else, but it all catches up eventually. Here, at the end of the corridor.

Mum sits down on a green chair by the wall.

'I'll wait here,' she says and points to the door that I am supposed to open.

'Aren't you coming in with me?' I ask.

'Best you go in first and I'll join you in a bit,' she says, with a weird expression. Like her face is twitching, maybe from laughter, or tears that aren't coming out properly. 'Let them know. That I'll be in soon, so they're ready for me. Off you go.'

She waves her hand to tell me to go inside but I hesitate. I don't want any of this. Oh god, I just want to go back to the island. To Ruth, Grandpa, the boat, the heat . . .

'Did you know . . .' I say. 'Did you know that a new-born sperm whale weighs one tonne?'

'Go on, Vinga,' she says.

She hugs me tight. Behind her are large windows that look out onto the hospital grounds. Branches and rubbish are strewn everywhere, broken signs and gutter pipes. But in here it is quiet. Like after the storm. Just a gentle murmur and the occasional child crying in the distance. Footsteps echoing somewhere far away, a coffee machine humming.

Now I'm just going to go up to the door and knock, that's all. That's all.

Mum found out first. They didn't say anything to me, but I noticed straight away that something was up.

Some evenings Mum didn't say a word. She just sat there at the table staring into space. Dinner was ready-made soup. I must have said one day that I didn't mind tomato soup, if I could get some mozzarella in it. But then it was all we ever had. And not even with mozzarella. It made clearing up really easy too.

After dinner Mum would shut herself in her bedroom and stay there until she came out and announced it was time for bed, and then suddenly it was a big rush. She got into a kind of frenzy.

Those evenings always ended with her sitting on the edge of my bed and apologising.

'Dear Vinga,' she said. 'Dear Vinga, forgive me, this is just so fucking hard.'

'I know,' I said.

Then she cried. Then I cried.

But there were other times when she would bounce around the flat playing really loud music. Those old songs she loved.

Since you left my mirror has forgotten what you looked like, now it will never see you again . . .

She would clean and tidy and pack and sing at the top of her lungs:

Everyone's forgotten, but not me, all I see reminds me of you . . .

Then we went on a trip and took the tram to Saltholmen to sit on the rocks in the early spring sun and eat salmon sandwiches. Mum closed her eyes with the sun on her face and said that life was good.

'Life is good now, Vinga.'

She said that all the time.

Or:

'It's always going to be like this, isn't it? Promise me. We'll stay this way for ever.'

'Isn't life great at the moment?'

'We'll remember this time for the rest of our lives, I know we will.'

I nodded, closed my eyes with the sun on my face and tried. But my stomach ached and the horizon was so very far away. I was supposed to be somewhere else.

Far in the distance, ships trawled silent waters. Far in the distance were ice bergs and plastic-bergs.

Far in the distance was the island. My summer island.

Mum found out first, but then it was my turn.

Dad came home to see us one weekend morning. Mum had bought green smoothies and peanut butter. The flat was vacuumed and the spring sun shone in through freshly cleaned windows. It was the first time we had been able to sit out on the balcony. The sun was warm, the birds were singing.

But if Dad was growing tomatoes again, then they were on a balcony in the city centre. I wondered, but didn't dare ask. I didn't even know if they had a balcony there.

When Dad and I went inside Mum cleared the table and tidied the kitchen. Dad didn't do that kind of thing at our place any more. And Mum had moved everything around in the cupboards so he couldn't have anyway.

Then we sat on the sofa. I wanted to go out but wasn't allowed. There was something Dad wanted to tell me, he said, but he wanted to wait until Mum could join us. It took ages. And when she eventually came in Dad went to the kitchen to get more coffee, but it was finished, Mum said, so Dad tried to brew a fresh pot but couldn't find any filters.

'I'll do it,' Mum said, so we had to sit there and wait for her again.

'Well, Vinga,' Dad said when Mum was back and they both had full, steaming cups of coffee. 'Well, there's something . . . I don't really know how you . . . or I . . . uh . . .'

Then it came:

'You're going to have a little brother or sister.'

I just stared at them. Dad came closer and put his arm around me. He looked like he was waiting for something. I stared at Mum instead. My skin started to crawl. My stomach flipped and my heart turned over. Nothing was as it should be.

'Isn't that exciting!?' said Mum.

But she said it much too loudly and her eyes were moist. She was sitting bolt upright and seemed so tense and stiff.

Obviously I knew it wasn't their baby. Angelica would be the one to carry it and be all glowing and then give birth to it. She would be the one to go round all smug with a pram and babble in baby talk with my little sibling. Or my . . . could it really be *my* anything?

'OK,' I said.

And then: 'Shit.'

I didn't mean to say that, it just came out. Shit.

I knew – they reminded me, but I remembered anyway – that I used to nag them for a baby sibling when I was little. And they had always given each other this weird look and said we'll see.

I could tell Dad thought, or at least wished and hoped in his heart of hearts, that I would be happy. That this would be a dream come true for me.

Fat fucking chance.

Dad could tell I wasn't happy so he just started talking, talking, talking.

He promised that everything was going to be just great and this absolutely wouldn't mean he had less time for me, quite the opposite, totally the opposite, because he'd have time off work to be with the baby so we could do everything together and we could meet after school and . . .

'But what about her?' I asked. 'Angelica?'

Then he went quiet.

'When is it due?' Mum asked.

'Ah yes, in autumn,' said Dad.

'But when?'

'September, maybe August. Well, probably more like August, but you never really know . . .'

'But . . .' said Mum in that loud voice again, standing up and beginning to pace. 'But . . . August is hardly autumn, is it?'

Dad said that Angelica was starting to show, but we'd stopped listening. We thought he should leave.

I wanted to be alone.

But we were going on an outing, Mum said.

'So you really should leave now,' she said, staring at Dad.

And I watched him through the window as he walked away through the park. I guessed Angelica was sitting there at Cafe Zenith wondering how it had gone.

'How did she take it?' she would ask. 'Was she happy?'

I guessed she was sitting there, at my and Dad's table, with a bulging belly, gold earrings, and a nice cup of tea.

I didn't wave.

Mum cried.

I refused to go with her on this outing.

My little brother is round and red. He is kicking his legs back and forth over the crumpled blanket. His fingers claw and rub and scratch at his flaky face. His eyes are closed but his frowning eyebrows make him look distressed and his mouth is moving a lot. He is lying on Dad's chest and Dad is patting his little thatch of black hair saying: 'There there, there there.'

But it doesn't help. It starts with a whimper then turns into a scream. Angelica is there in a flash to steal him away. My little brother. She smiles at me briefly and sort of waves hello with her eyes, but then she is lying in bed right up close to Dad. Her huge breasts spill out and my little brother latches on and quietens down.

Then Dad gets up. He is in his underwear and he smells funny when we hug. Sweat and flesh.

'Darling Vinga,' he says. 'Darling Vinga, how I've missed you.'

I think they should have got dressed and aired the place out a bit. They knew I was coming. But they're literally glowing and I don't want to get in the way.

Is this what I've come here for? To sit on dirty sheets surrounded by the smell of flesh and blood and naked bodies? If it were up to me I would have stayed on the island. I was going to come home eventually anyway. For autumn and trams and obligations.

But I didn't get a choice. Mum had already made up her mind when she called: I was coming home, and Grandpa was coming with me, even though he didn't want to either. And we did what she said. It was for her sake.

I've missed Dad, of course I have, but I'm not sure about

any of this. It's just all so weird. So new and so weird.

I look over at the bed where that baby is suckling. The baby brother I didn't really want. All I see is a fuzzy little neck moving slowly.

My brother? A person?

'What's his name going to be?' I ask.

I want, but don't dare, to go over to them. He is lying there, so close to her body. It's like Angelica is everywhere, filling up the whole room.

'We're not really sure. What do you think?'

'Dunno. Karl-Alfred, maybe. Or Fritiof.'

Angelica giggles and Dad smiles.

'Well, we'll see,' he says. 'Where's Mum?'

It feels weird that he calls her that. Mum.

'She's sitting outside. Might come in a bit.'

Dad understands and starts getting dressed. Angelica pulls up the blanket and hides Karl-Alfred underneath.

Like she's scared of her coming in. *Mum*.

Then we sit there, me and Dad, and when my little brother has finished breastfeeding, Angelica brings him to us. My little brother. Or whoever he is.

We sit on the bed and I hold him on my lap as he sleeps. Completely still now, with his arms hanging down over my thighs. His legs are like a frog's. Only his tongue moves a bit inside those thick lips. He barely has a chin, it's more like a gap – could there be something wrong with him?

Angelica lies down with her back to us. She needs to rest, Dad says, she's had a tough time, he says, but I really don't want to think about it.

He looks dishevelled, Dad. Dishevelled and happy, but tears run down his face as he looks at me and strokes my back, then he kisses me on the head.

'This is your little brother. You're going to take good care of him, aren't you?'

I don't know how to answer. He can take care of his own baby without me. But I do want to. Don't I?

'He has your lips,' says Dad. 'I can see the family resemblance.'

The lips, yes.

Then he asks about the island and I tell him about the boat and the heat and the birds. I tell him about the Sand Witch and the porpoise and the rhubarb lemonade. The smell of pipe tobacco and the sound of the rosefinch: '*Pleased to meet you, pleased to meet you . . .*'

I tell him in English and then translate into Swedish: 'Pleased to meet you.'

'You too,' Dad says and laughs so hard he makes the bed and baby shake.

I can't stop thinking about those enormous breasts. They must be shaking too. Full of milk. I don't know why but it seems kind of gross.

And then I tell him about Ruth.

Not everything, of course, just that I made a friend. One who is totally different. I can feel myself getting hot when I talk about her, but it doesn't matter this time, and I decide I'd rather tell him first than have to answer a bunch of questions. I don't care if he can tell. Well, not much anyway.

Dad smiles.

He squeezes my hand hard and says he's so happy I've been

having a good time. But he doesn't make a big deal about me having a friend. Doesn't say, 'Oh wow, how exciting, tell me more,' like Mum always does.

He just says he's glad I've been having a good time. No advice on what to do or how to act, none of that.

'Good,' he says.

And then he says that he's glad I came.

'I've really missed you, you know,' he says.

He looks at me. His eyes look sadder, softer, serious.

'You should know that . . .'

But then Mum is standing in the doorway.

'Would you believe this storm!?' she laughs, but it comes out sounding very unnatural.

Mum leans over and gives Angelica a hug. I wasn't even sure whether they'd met before.

'Congratulations,' she says. 'Well done.'

She sounds so perky and cheery. So fake.

It makes my stomach hurt to hear it. Sometimes I get annoyed at Mum's fake happiness. But at the same time I feel sorry for her. I hate feeling sorry for her.

Then she comes over to me and Dad sitting on the edge of the bed. She crouches down, looks at the little one and gives him a gentle pat.

Then she hugs me hard, hard, hard, and Dad a bit more softly.

She puts down the flowers she has been carrying around on that little cart between the beds. Then she tells me she'll be waiting outside. She dashes out the door but we see her burst into sobs the moment she turns around.

Dad calls after her, but the door slams shut and she is gone.

Afterwards everything feels so quiet and calm, despite the wind still bristling in the trees and clouds racing across the sky.

We sit on the bus, Mum and me, and it feels good to see the hospital get smaller and smaller behind us. In one of its rooms Dad is still lying there between crumpled bedsheets and Karl-Alfred is being fed from Angelica's exhausted body. My brother. With my lips.

I don't know my little brother's mother.

She doesn't know me. Maybe never will.

'Why did you cry?' I ask.

'Oh, it's just so weird,' Mum says. She takes a deep breath and quickly wipes away the little tear squeezing its way out.

She swallows. Takes another deep breath and swallows.

'It's so weird seeing you with a little brother. A newborn baby that is in no way mine. You know, I've missed you so much these past few weeks. I regretted letting you go by yourself, but you've had a good time, haven't you?'

'Yes, it is weird. That Dad . . . is lying there now. With a . . . with a . . . a . . . new family.'

'Weird, yes. So bloody fucking weird.'

Mum laughs, then turns to look out the window. I assume more tears are coming. And it would only get worse if she looked at me. Worse if she spoke.

But she carries on. They're a bit shaky, the words, but she carries on:

'But you know what?' she says. 'You know what? We've got each other. You and I still have each other. And we still have him. We are still a family. Well, we are, aren't we?'

My stomach turns.

She says it again. That we're still a family, just a little different now.

'Yes, a little different,' she continues. 'But he loves you just as much, you know that. And he and I both have you, and there's no changing that.'

'Nope, you'll never be rid of me,' I say and she laughs.

She laughs and cries and the bus rocks in the wind. Outside I see tattered signs, newspapers and litter tumbling along the pavements and the few people who have braved the slightly calmer weather have to jump out of the way.

I tell Mum that if we're still some sort of family then I want them to act like it. We should go out for a pizza, like we used to. And then I'll go back to the island, so I can have a bit more time there before school begins.

'Oh sure,' she says simply. 'Sure, of course we can. And of course you can. If that's what you want.'

She does that sigh again.

'I'll miss you though.'

Then she starts laughing again. And so do I.

We are still laughing when we open the door to the flat and Grandpa asks us how it went.

'He's so small,' I say. 'My little brother is really small and he's going to be called Karl-Alfred and he has my lips.'

'The storm has calmed down,' Grandpa says that evening when we're having our tea. 'I think the boats will be running.'

And then I realise what he means. He's going home. And I'm staying. I've promised I would.

'OK,' I say shortly, looking down into my cup.

Then he coughs and I have to look up.

'Hey, captain. You'll join me soon enough.'

He sort of flutters his giant eyebrows around as he says it. I make an effort to appear sure. Feel tears well up.

'Yes,' I say. 'I'll join you soon.'

Then Grandpa gets up and goes to pack his chequered bag. He looks old in this flat. Old and worn-out somehow. Greyer. He needs the island, I think to myself, he can't live without the sea, the salt and the birds. I let him go and keep looking down in my empty teacup.

On the way to my room I stop at the big mirror in the hallway. I stand there and look at myself. My hair seems to have enjoyed the sun and saltwater; it's sticking out in all directions, like fire. I've outgrown my spotted nightdress since last spring and I can see my legs are freckly and covered in bruises. But they look strong somehow. Tough. Not quite as bandy and weird. It's all growing and changing. My face is red and puffy from sleep and tears, my lips are dry, a little cracked. Oh, those lips, so soft . . .

Grandpa is folding his clothes as I pass him. We ignore each other.

That evening I cry again. For Dad, who is so close but so far away, and Grandpa, who is about to go to the island. And for Mum, who will be alone again. And the coming autumn.

181

In the morning, when everything is ready and I am dressed and the bed is made, Grandpa knocks on the door. I glimpse Mum outside. Running around looking for something, as usual.

'Accompany me to the station?'

The clouds are still racing across the sky outside and the trees in the park are struggling to stay upright. But it's like something different is happening now. It's lighter.

We walk along, huddled against the wind, Mum and Grandpa and me. We pass by the shop where Dad and I used to buy ice cream after school when I was little. Through the park, where Kalle and I each had our own pirate ship before he moved to Arjeplog a million years ago. Past the bushes blooming with fragrant, white flowers, where Dad sometimes stood waiting for me, and past that little forest path down by the lake where I learned to ride a bike one day and Dad was there cheering and shouting; I still remember it so clearly. I had my cuddly rabbit Sune on the back rack. I loved Sune, who disappeared under mysterious circumstances when I started Year 4 or 5. What a disaster that was. My stomach still flips when I think of Sune and I could cry.

I take Grandpa's hand and walk along holding it. We very rarely do this normally, but it feels natural here.

And on the other side of the street I spy Cafe Zenith.

Where I first met Angelica. That scarf and its smell.

None of us talk, though Mum tries.

Mum and I make sure Grandpa gets on the right train, then she asks for the third time if he's got his sandwiches. I ask about his pipe. I haven't seen him smoke since he left the island.

'That stayed behind,' he says. 'There's enough smoke on the mainland already.'

Then he gives me a big hug and Mum gets one too. Then he sends his regards to Dad and that little one and says when I come out to the island again we'll have crab.

When I come again.

Dad's changed. He always used to order the vegetarian pizza, minus olives. Now he's sitting at the table and browsing the menu and muttering.

'Maybe I should go for a *frutti di mare*,' he says eventually. 'After all, this is a real celebration.'

Mum and I look at him in surprise.

'It's got mussels on it,' says Mum.

'And cockles,' I say, and think of Ruth.

'Yes, Christ, I know what *frutti di mare* means,' says Dad. 'Fruit salad from the sea.'

'Well, not exactly salad, but sure,' says Mum.

Now we're sitting in a restaurant, the whole family. And Dad orders a *frutti di mare* and a large beer, and Mum gets a napolitana and a large beer. I get a margherita and a cola.

Candles on the table. A football match on TV, no sound. We're practically the only ones here, us and that friendly pizza chef with the moustache. He seems to recognise us, even though it's been a while. He smiles at least, but he might smile at everyone.

He'd better not even think about giving me a lollipop.

'So you've started eating meat all of a sudden? And shellfish – you hate shellfish?!'

Mum stares at Dad.

'All of a sudden? Well . . .' he says. 'Can't get stuck in old ways.'

Mum just scoffs.

Then we sit there and talk about everything under the sun. About Grandpa and the island, about Mum's job, about Angelica and Karl-Alfred.

'Except he might have a different name,' says Dad. 'Angelica likes Charlie.'

He looks at us anxiously, like he wants our opinion, but is afraid of what it might be. He wants our approval.

Mum looks tired and says she doesn't think it's really our business.

'But it's not the most beautiful name I've ever heard,' she says.

I almost scream at Dad that Charlie is wrong!

'Under no circumstances,' I blurt out.

That's what he always says when he is putting his foot down.

'But it's almost like a nickname for Karl-Alfred,' Dad ventures.

'It's ugly,' I say, and Mum agrees.

'Awful, actually.'

Finally Dad admits he has also had a hard time getting used to the idea of Charlie.

'Doesn't it sound more like a dog's name?' he whispers, as if someone might hear.

'Yes,' says Mum. 'One of those little rat dogs, what are they called . . . ?'

'Chihuahuas,' I say and suddenly feel like it's the three of us again.

All three of us on one team against Angelica and everyone else. Now it's us three that agree. Charlie is a chihuahua that you nearly trip over in town. And we laugh about it.

Then we talk a bit about Ruth.

They ask me things and I look at them and they smile at

each other across the table and Dad calls for another round of beers and cola and insists we stay a little longer. He's having a good time now. And just because he looks so happy and because he and Mum are laughing together, I let them carry on. They ask and I answer. But I don't say anything about the kiss. I don't say anything about how my whole body reacts to the mere sound of her name.

That I've kissed someone. They'd never believe it.

And no one mentions autumn. No one says anything about my new school or new room. No one says that everything is going to be OK. No one promises anything.

Because it's all right for now. Right now it's actually really fucking great sitting here.

It's almost dark when we emerge from the restaurant. Several families have come in and the pizza chef is busy. He just waves and smiles. It occurs to me that it might be the last time he sees the three of us together.

When we say goodbye Mum and Dad hug and before he gets on the tram he takes me in his arms and sort of scoops me up as if I were all little and newborn. Just for this evening, he can do that.

'I love you Vinga,' he whispers in my ear. 'Promise you'll come home soon.'

Home.

Tears spring to my eyes and I wave stupidly at the tram that's about to take him to the city centre and the balcony with tomato plants and my little brother and his happy mother.

I still haven't seen my new room.

On the way home I sing quietly to myself.
What fun we had at the party,
How I wish I could have stayed there.

The Maiden Voyage

Finally.

Now we're back at the table, tossing pieces of crab shell into a basket in the corner. I'll give them to the birds later.

Now he pours himself another drink – 'For Karl-Alfred,' he says – and his pipe is waiting on the table. Now we're mainly just keeping our mouths shut and are perfectly content.

Now it's the shipping forecast. Now it's summer again, without a cloud in the sky, but the plants have had rain now and are happy. Now it's just the usual sea birds flying around and the sailor's caps hanging on their hooks.

Now Grandpa's suit is hanging up there under the stairs waiting for our next evening at the pub. Now Grandpa is getting the chess board out. Now he thinks it's time I won a game, but once again it ends up with him looking up at me disappointedly saying, 'Checkmate,' and I'm left scratching my head.

Now we open the door out to the garden just to enjoy the scents a little. Now one of the sheep bleats from behind the shed.

Now all is how it should be.

Then morning comes and everything is as usual. Grandpa is sitting at the table and listening to the radio when I get up. The porridge is already bubbling on the stove. The sun is already high in a clear blue sky and it's hot again.

Grandpa mumbles, 'Good morning,' and turns down the radio. Yes, everything is as usual.

And we eat breakfast without any small talk and I go out to pee and watch the birds in the lilac bush. Try to name them: blue tit, great tit, linnet . . . but in truth I have no idea.

We potter around the house for a while before Grandpa says we should go down to check how the boat has survived the storm. Of course we should.

No sooner do we reach the steps than I see her. Slender, all in black. The one Grandpa calls an angel.

Ruth.

How I have longed for her. She has been here inside me the whole time and I've just been waiting until I could see her again.

But still, I'm nervous about how it will go.

Ruth is standing by the boat and waving. I look back at Grandpa who is walking behind me. Then he shows me that smile of his.

My heart starts racing and I feel a warmth in the belly, and a tickling sensation. For all the possibilities. All that eternity and infinity.

I look back at Grandpa again and he nods and I start to run.

My feet have already lost their familiarity with the round pebbles and shells and it hurts as I run. But I don't care.

Let them bleed if they want.

I run to the boat and to Ruth and I see that she is smiling. It's strange seeing her again, like we don't really know what to say, but she reaches out her hand and sort of pats me on the arm like everything is exactly how it's always been. But I see something different in her smile.

And then Grandpa is there.

'So. Shall we show her then?' he says.

To Ruth.

She nods and together they pull the tarpaulin off the boat.

I just stare. I remember exactly how far I'd got when I left the island. I know exactly how much there was left to do. And now I look at the boat and can't see anything else that needs doing. I feel Grandpa and Ruth looking at me and waiting for some sort of reaction, but all I can do is stare. Yep, I just stand there wide-eyed and stare.

A long time passes, then Grandpa speaks:

'I think it's time for the maiden voyage.'

I am happy, of course. Happy about the boat, but my head is in a spin. Grandpa and Ruth are standing there on the pebbly beach, looking at me and at each other and smiling in some secret way. Then they tell me what happened.

It turns out that Grandpa had gone straight to Ruth as soon as he returned to the island and asked for her help in making the boat seaworthy. As a surprise for me.

And then they spent three days, from dawn to dusk, as Grandpa says, working and toiling away.

Ruth tells me the Sand Witch kept them company and they fed it with egg sandwiches.

And I am happy, but at the same time . . . Them two?

Ruth was like my secret. Someone only I knew. I'm finding it hard to get my head around. What did they talk about, if they talked at all? Grandpa, that weird old man, and Ruth, an odd pair, for my sake . . .

'We've had a lot of fun,' says Grandpa.

'Actually it's been really tough going,' says Ruth, which is good to hear. 'He's a bloody slave driver, this one.'

She nods to Grandpa.

A prison guard and a slave driver, then.

'Fun,' Grandpa mumbles again and tries to smooth his hair back.

We rig up the boat, fix the mast and raise the sail. All the rope ends need threading and fastening. Then Grandpa shows us where Ylva has come with her tractor and dropped a few logs so we can sort of pull the boat down, like on a ramp, straight into the water. It is still very heavy, almost impossible. And

Ruth just stands there with her arms by her side and doesn't even bother trying.

'Come on,' Grandpa says to her as he pushes and pulls.

She sighs and when she does come to help it doesn't really make a difference.

Finally we get the boat bobbing on the water anyway. We have to wade out a bit and then it's super hard to get in over the side. My tough old Grandpa does it anyway and makes it look easy.

'Aren't you coming?' I call to Ruth.

But she shakes her head and looks at me with fear in her eyes.

'Come on, you know I hate the sea. I'll wait here.'

Then we look at each other, Grandpa and me, and laugh.

And then we're sitting there and bobbing on a calm sea. There is barely any wind. And there was me dreaming of sailing into the horizon and just sort of carrying on . . . But we stay in earshot of that thin, dark figure standing on land under her drooping hat.

'Waiting for wind,' mumbles Grandpa and he starts humming a tune.

One day the sea was a desert before my eyes
Not a bird to be seen flying in the skies

The sail is just hanging there in the baking sun. It isn't long before we feel sort of like shipwreck survivors who have to row back to land.

But it's a maiden voyage nevertheless.

After that I go out sailing nearly every day. We've fixed it so the boat can stay moored on the shoreline.

'As long as it stays calm like this,' Grandpa said, gazing out at the sea and sky.

And nearly every day Ruth sits on the beach and waits for me. Sometimes I look at the shore and see her, a black dot on the rocks. She climbs up and down, to the lighthouse and back. It looks terribly dangerous, but when I sail into shore she is always there, alive and well, to greet me.

Then I get that funny feeling in my stomach. Someone is waiting for me. Someone wants to be with me. This has never happened before, not like this.

Things have calmed down on the mainland since the storm. Those Italian and Polish firefighters have gone home, but barbecues are still banned. My insides still smoulder and blaze, but more gently now.

Then we walk along the beach together and kick about in the pebbles and shells.

Ruth still complains a lot, it's kind of her thing. Complains about everything she can't do here. Everything she doesn't have. How her granny forces her to work and how great it is back in the city.

That there is no proper internet on this godforsaken island.

Her words are like a punch in the belly. All the best things I can possibly imagine aren't good enough for her.

And every time we walk along the beach she tells me things about her life in the city, though I'm not sure I want to know.

And she laughs when I tell her about my little brother and doesn't get what I have against the name Charlie.

'What? It's super cute,' she says and then says she'd like to meet him. She asks if we're alike.

'Not really,' I say. 'But he has my lips.'

'Good,' she replies simply, then we stop at the bottom of the steps and hug tight before going our separate ways.

I say we'll see each other tomorrow or maybe up on the cliff this evening; she can always come to our house if she wants. But she just says we'll see and I think she means about everything. Then I just nod. And go.

I don't turn back to wave. I just disappear up the steps to the house and to Grandpa and everything is exactly as it should be. It's actually quite nice to be alone sometimes too.

It's a pretty perfect ending to the story of this summer. But it doesn't end here.

Grandpa

Ruth and I find him.

It's afternoon and the heat is intense. The birds are sitting still, like they're in a museum, and the water and sky are one motionless blue expanse. The air is heavy, sweat is pouring, we walk slowly up the steps, to the white house.

Ruth rarely comes with me but right now it's a question of life and death. We're in desperate need of some of Grandpa's rhubarb lemonade.

Grandpa is napping on a blanket under the lilac bush when we arrive. He does that a lot these days.

'Hey Grandpa, we're just going to get some rhubarb lemonade.'

'Shush, he's sleeping,' Ruth says and laughs as if I've done something really weird.

Inside the house the radio is on and some rescue leader is saying that they did all they could and then there's a politician and then an angry forester.

Ruth sees the chess board still on the table from last night. White in checkmate, as always.

'Do you play?' asks Ruth.

'Only with Grandpa.'

'Wow, that's so cool. Shall we play a game?'

And I realise this means I do know at least one other person who plays.

'This evening?' I ask.

'OK.'

Ruth stands there looking at the board as if she can track every move we made. I'm a bit intimidated; she might be really good.

I take the jug out of the fridge and three glasses and go out and sit down next to Grandpa.

'Grandpa,' I say and touch his shoulder. 'Grandpa, do you want some?'

I look up at the house and see Ruth in the doorway. She is standing there on the front step with her hair in her face and her eyes wide open. She looks terrified.

Then something tightens deep down inside.

I lift the sailor's cap lying over Grandpa's eyes and pat him on the cheek and feel how clammy it is.

'Grandpa?'

Now Ruth is beside me, bending down over Grandpa. Then she slaps him in the face.

'What the hell are you doing?!' I shout and the tears have already started to flow, my heart is racing, fast and hard.

'But, Vinga. Don't you see. He's not waking up.'

'No, because he's a really deep sleeper!' I scream. 'He's always like this. He's sleeping. Let him sleep!'

'He's not sleeping, Vinga,' Ruth says very calmly. 'He's dead.'

Then I hear the rosefinch. Not just any bird. It's that one. I know it shouldn't be singing this late in summer, that's what Grandpa has said, but I hear it, I know I do!

'I'll go and get Ylva,' says Ruth.

'I'll be quick,' she says.

But all I hear is *Pleased to meet you.*

Then I lie there, with my head on Grandpa's shoulder, soaking his shirt with my tears. His chest isn't moving. It's as still as the sea below. Everything is still. The sheep are standing in their field and staring, and the sun is blazing as usual. Sunlight filters through the branches of the lilac bush and creates flecks of light on Grandpa's body. The sun touches everything, but I am cold. Shivering, freezing and crying.

The rosefinch is very close, piercing my ears.

Pleased to meet you.

I lie there and hope it takes a long time for Ylva and Ruth to come. Or whoever.

Because right now I am with Grandpa. And never will be again.

Now I am with Grandpa for the last time.

Even though the body lying next to me is lifeless, I can feel him here.

'Grandpa,' I whisper. 'Grandpa.'

And I know he can hear. He has to.

'Grandpa, what would I have done without you, this summer?' I whisper, thankful that no one else is listening.

Still, I whisper again.

'Grandpa. Thank you.'

When the sound of the quad bike approaches I hold onto Grandpa as hard as I can and run my hand over his prickly cheeks. I kiss him on the lips, which are cold and dead. But they are his.

Then I scream. Scream loud.

I lie there screaming until I feel Ruth's thin arms around me and Ylva slowly comes over and feels Grandpa.

'Bengtsson will be here any minute,' she said and takes off her hat. Fat tears roll down her cheeks and fall into the dry yellow grass.

Bengtsson is the doctor.

As if she could do anything.

And now the rosefinch has gone quiet or gone away or died.

Mum came that same evening.

I spent all day sitting in Ylva's kitchen with that burnt smell and thought about all the times we had been there, me and Grandpa, to call Mum.

Sit and talk.

Ylva was making an effort but all I could do was cry. Ruth was there. She sat next to me on the kitchen bench with her arms around me.

I just cried and couldn't stop and kept thinking over and over that it couldn't be true. It must be a dream. But then I kept realising over and over again that it was true and then I felt something like panic in my body and I just wanted to scream.

That evening Ylva took me on her quad bike down to the harbour and the boat. It was the last boat of the day and night was falling. When we pulled out of Ylva's farm and passed the Great Wood I turned around and caught a glimpse of Grandpa's little white house. The low evening sun was glittering; it looked so alive.

The wind in our faces made my eyes water and the birds took flight from the bushes.

'Oh sweetheart, it should never have happened this way.'

That was the first thing Mum said before we threw our arms around each other and clung tight. I couldn't answer. And I couldn't give a shit about her calling me sweetheart. What did it matter now.

Ylva stood beside us looking very sad. The old men who passed by mumbled things and took off their hats. Even that shiny-buttoned captain came ashore and took my hand.

'Condolences,' he said. 'He certainly was a true seaman.'

Not like you then, I thought, but said nothing.

Yes, everyone seemed sad. Everyone was mourning. Everyone knew that my Grandpa was dead. Dead.

That evening there was no shipping forecast. That evening there was no pipe, no tea. We just went to bed, me and Mum in Grandpa's bed, with dirty sheets that smelled like tobacco.

That evening it was impossible to sleep.

'Dad sends all his love,' whispered Mum, her mouth right up to my ear.

'Mm.'

'He misses you and is thinking about you all the time,' she said.

'Why isn't he here then?'

'Remember your little brother?'

'Mm, Karl-Alfred.'

She laughed.

'I'm afraid it looks like he's going to have that dog name after all.'

I couldn't believe it. Not Charlie! A goddamn little chihuahua. And after I'd actually made my mind up to like that little brother with the same fat little kissable lips as me.

I will never call him anything other than Karl-Alfred. Angelica can say what she likes.

After that I must have fallen asleep somehow.

There was a funeral later.

But first there was a bunch of things to organise and Mum spent a lot of time at Ylva's house with the phone glued to her ear. People from the village kept coming over to tell us how sorry they were.

It was tiring.

Ruth came too. But we didn't talk about Grandpa much – hardly at all. We played chess.

We moved the little wooden table round the back of the house, to be near the lilac bush and other usual things. We sat there at the table and played. We were pretty much at the same level and I don't know if Ruth was letting me win because she felt bad for me, but it was almost always me who said checkmate. I wasn't used to it.

Sometimes the tears came and I let them. It was only Ruth there after all.

Well, Grandpa got use out of his whole suit at last. Complete with tie and fancy mainland shoes. He was buried with his sailor's cap on.

The whole island was there and the little church was packed. Some people had to stand. I didn't know there were so many people on the island. And that they all had smart clothes hanging somewhere in their little cottages.

I sat in between Mum and Ruth and went through three of Grandpa's cloth handkerchiefs. So much snot, so many tears.

When everyone else stood up and sang, I stayed seated.

'It's OK,' said Mum. 'You can sit.'

Teach me, trees, to die with grace

When yellow leaves take green leaves' place
Until a richer spring shall be
And my mighty living tree shall stand,
With roots deep in the fertile land,
In the summer of eternity.

Then Ruth cried too. Her granny snorted like a pig when she cried.

Then we went up to the coffin to say a final goodbye. Mum stood there for a long time and patted the white wood and mumbled something to her father that no one else could hear.

I put Grandpa's pipe in his coffin and tried to whistle *Pleased to meet you*, but it mainly just came out as tears and snot, tears and snot.

Dad wasn't there. I spoke to him on the phone afterwards and he promised that the baby's name wasn't decided for sure yet.

'Because he can't be called that,' I said.

'I hope you know I'm thinking about you,' he said.

'Sure,' I said.

'Your room is nearly ready now,' he said.

'OK,' I said.

Then there was coffee in that barn that was sometimes a pub. Everyone wanted to talk to Mum and there was a sort of sad, quiet mumble everywhere. It was much better before when people drank beer and Ylva stood behind the bar.

Ruth and I sat in the furthest corner, in the same place I saw her for the first time.

I watched Mum who was standing not far away with her coffee cup. She suddenly looked very old standing there surrounded by islanders dressed in smart clothes and with their hair combed, for once. With no Grandpa beside her. He should have been standing there, getting annoyed at the small talk, but now it was just her. She had lost her father, gone for ever, it was so awful. At least my father was somewhere on the other side of the sea and I could talk to him on the phone . . .

Suddenly Ruth poked me and nodded at the door and the summer sea glittering outside. We slowly crept out and went down to the harbour. Arm in arm.

There wasn't a soul in the village. Everyone was at the funeral. The shop was closed and there was only a handful of confused tourists reading the bulletin board.

We sat there by the harbour and stared, Ruth and me, and I wondered what life would be like from now on. In the autumn. In the city. Where she had her friends and her climbing and everything.

I didn't ask. Just sat in silence wondering and holding her hand in mine.

There is no summer of eternity. Summers end and autumn comes with its red leaves and biting cold and darkness in the city park. Dreams of the non-existent sea outside school windows.

This summer is also coming to an end. Eventually we will take the boat to that bloody mainland and drive home. Then it'll be all new rooms and so-called classmates and little brothers. Grown-ups prattling on about after-school activities and book recommendations. Then everything will be different.

And out on the island the sailing boat will be lying under a tarp all lonely and abandoned like a lost cuddly rabbit called Sune.

This summer might have been the worst ever. But it has also been the best. And now it is over.

Grandpa has a gravestone.

Here rests a sailor.

I thought the word 'rests' sounded weird, basically a lie, but Mum decided that's what it should say.

I will never be able to express how much I miss Grandpa. Mum said I'll get used to it, that's the good thing about humans, we can always get used to anything.

'Except a stone in your shoe,' I said.

Mum understood and smiled.

'Here lies a stone in your shoe,' the gravestone should have said, because I will never ever get used to him not being around.

It's my last evening on the island and I am sitting here on the cliff.

I have my sailor's cap on my head and my heart in the right place. I sit gazing out over the sea, looking into infinity. It's comforting to know I could take out my boat and just keep going, disappear.

Grandpa would be with me. He is out there somewhere with the whales and giant squid. The sailor.

Sailor of eternity.

Ylva has promised to keep an eye on the boat.

Mum is in the house cleaning out the last bits.

Next year we can stay here all summer holiday, she has promised. I think I want to, but I don't know what it will be like without Grandpa. So empty. And what about Dad? Would he come? Angelica, Karl-Alfred? I doubt she would come.

Ylva is going to take care of the house and garden for now anyway, and she is going to put fresh flowers on Grandpa's grave.

Ruth left yesterday. We walked down to the boat a little way behind the others, me and her.

'See you back in the city,' she said, and I just thought, *We'll see*. Then we kissed.

She pulled me into her, behind one of the bushes along the road, by the bench where the old men usually sit. She grabbed my arm and suddenly there we were behind the dense greenery and she held me so tight and I hugged her back and there were butterflies in my stomach and my cheeks got hot. Soft lips pressed together and open mouths and warm tongues meeting. I can hardly believe we dared. Anyone might have seen. I was terrified. I could hear my own heartbeat.

When we emerged from our hiding place the others were already standing by the harbour and looking around for us, worried.

And then there we were. In the blazing sun, dripping sweat. Our hair and lips dishevelled and our hearts pumping blood.

We walked along hand in hand. She in her black hat and baggy shirt. Me in my leopard-print shorts and sailor's shirt.

'I'll call you, I promise!'

'Sure,' I said and watched the boat sail away from the harbour.

No albatross by the lighthouse, but that evening the rain came.

And the tears.

When I leave my spot up here on the cliff and go down to Mum and the house, everything is wet. No sea shanties.

And life on the island just carries on. The old men are sitting on their benches in their trousers and braces, the sheep are still chewing away. People gossip at the pub on Wednesdays, the birds continue to sing.

But far out to sea the whales are swimming along the surface without anyone to witness them. They are simply there, though no one knows.

And the giant squid. Quick flashes of light somewhere in all that darkness.

Acknowledgements

Thank you Hedvig for reading to the end.
Thank you Lennart Sjögren for *The Bird Hunters*.

Oskar Kroon

Oskar Kroon was a journalist who retrained as a baker. Now he writes full-time so he can spend time with his family. *Rhubarb Lemonade* was published in Sweden in 2019 as *Waiting for Wind* and won the August Prize for the best Swedish children's book in 2019. It has been published in twelve other languages.

HOT
KEY
BOOKS

Thank you for choosing a Hot Key book.

If you want to know more about our authors and what we publish, you can find us online.

You can start at our website

www.hotkeybooks.com

And you can also find us on:

We hope to see you soon!